THE
WIZARDS
OF
WWII

(ROYAL AIR FORCE –
THE BATTLE OF BRITAIN)

BY

BENJAMIN ROBERT WEBB

1st EDITION

PUBLISHED BY TEMPORAL ZOETROPE

ISBN-13: 978-1548770853
ISBN-10: 154877085X

FOR
JAMES

CHAPTERS

1

ONE FINE DAY

IN THE MIDDLE OF THE NIGHT

If I remember correctly, this story, albeit my story, the story of that part I was to play in the aerial confrontation of blood and guts and lost stones and bones that came to be known after the fact, as The Battle of Britain, starts one fine day in the middle of the night; for it was the night of the seventeenth of May, 1940, a night that turned out to be a very special night indeed.

A night upon which the moon was full, and though there were clouds in the sky on this night, none of them were touching upon the majesty of the face of the full moon, between the light of which, and the silver lining of those clouds as bright as the moon itself, for it was nought but the moon's own light these clouds were stealing, and thus silently serenading this serenity of a silent illumined song right back at the night itself in full; because of this orchestration of moonlight, the one source working in accord with the other, the black of this night on earth was not black, but blue, a deep dark midnight-blue; and the stars, though every square inch of night sky, of which there was exposed a hundred thousand crystal clear midnight-blue acres thereof, wherever the cloud acres on this night had not been farmed, was surely teeming with just such as that, stars without count, the stars on this night could not be seen for the blue of this night denied the sky its distant twinkle, but for maybe one or two; blue-white diamonds these things, glistening and glowing in the inky midnight-blue of this damn near perfect mid-summer's night on earth; such as was, though I couldn't know it at the time, for little could I know at the time, where those things I'd very soon be taking for granted were concerned, this night on earth was, the very eve of my introduction to the war.

I couldn't have dreamed of a more perfect night.

Nor could anyone, not even a master of the still life paintbrush, have painted such as this still life night on earth, and done such as this night, in all of its silver-aligned splendor, any justice to its beauty at all, bar no master who ever lived. For though masters there were once upon a time, and so much so, such masters as there were, were surely ten-a-penny and to be found like pigeons on any given day of the week, gathered in the park with their easels under their arms, in search of that one commission it might just take them the rest of their life to complete, none ever mastered the medium of moonlight to such a degree, as to be said to be, after the fact, a master proficient in the art of illustrated moonshine, moonlight, moonbeams, mooncankers, moonhoofs, and moonglow; such as makes snowbanks of clouds, worth their weight in silver if not sixpence on the sketch but only be it signed by their maker. For only *he* paints in such pictures for vistas, in pastures as sublime as fields of moonlight.

For 'twas nought but a delicate brush in the steady hand of a master of the craft, that painted the clouds on this night, so perfectly lighting them for effect, with moon, or the moon with the light of the clouds for just to look, was just to see, when to see one truly would have needed to look into this scenic vista of a canvass unveiled upon the night as oft summering lovers might throw down upon the ground a blanket to picnic upon, and thus dine, so too now had such star-crossed lovers as the moon and the moonlight, thrown against the very backdrop of the sky, on this night on earth, such a blanket and a picnic with which to feast thy mind's imagination thereupon, both sweetly and deeply.

I ate my fill gladly.

But I did not take my fill, deeply.

Ever I am sure there would have proved more to see, had I only taken the time to actually look. But one could not look upon the world's everywhere all at once. Certainly not from my current vantage point, which was just my bedroom window, not that it actually was my bedroom, when it was just another guest room in the farmhouse I was staying at would be the more apt accurate description in line with the truth thereof, as to where I was at this time.

Not a praying man, nor ever a praying man, this night on

earth moved me, and shook my world like it had not been rocked since thy cradle came crashing down.

Two owls agreed, least it was just the one owl hooting twice? Even so, perfect it was. The owl, be it an owl, or owls, be it owls, only made it more perfect than it had been prior to this owl, or owls, sounding the still settled serenity of this night on earth that had, until the owls took notice of the silence, and shattered it, been broken by not even the stirrings of a field mouse, of which the meadows were no doubt teeming with thousands, but if at all any field mouse out there had been about to, or was thinking about breaking the silence themselves, once the owl, or owls, had sounded the night, everything else in the world as it seemed to me, thought better of trying to better such as an owl, especially be thee a field mouse.

Predatory thing is an owl.

So say the field mice.

Predatory thing is a field mouse.

So say the stalks of corn.

Perfect is the world, says one, says all.

Perfect that was, until I saw the dragon, and my brother didn't though both of us had been looking at the same moon at precisely the same time. And that was the truth of it on this night on earth, for there *had* been a dragon, and I saw it and my brother didn't, for he didn't have the eyes for such as dragons. No eyes at all for that kind of dreaming, for my brother, unlike I, was not much of a dreamer: My brother was a one for other things, more mundane things and ways of seeing such, I found, I always saw differently. The difference between us such, all can be easily best summed up with a simple Ages old observation of an adage that would say of the two of us, though siblings we were, whereas he was born to be the ruddy-muddy mundane scientist, with their ruddy-muddy mundane worldview, I was instead, for my part that is, in the greater mystery play that is life, born to be the sorcerer of the family.

Lucky for me, I guess, from the best of points of view, and lucky for my brother, but not really all things considered; given he died and I didn't upon this night on earth, under most unusual circumstances. But then again, at least he was spared the war, in the flesh so to speak, just not necessarily as you'll come to learn, in Spirit. The war didn't get my brother like it got me, pretty much because my brother didn't get the war like I got the war, and boy did I ever get the war I was looking for: Just the very war of late I'd been dreaming about.

It was from dreams of war that I was awoken on this night: The night my life was to be changed, not so much forever more, but at least for the next few months, which as it turned out, was all the time I had left of the life I had been living at the time.

I was seventeen years old, just, and that fight which came to be called The Battle of Britain was still at this time, a few months away from killing me.

I'd been dreaming of the old biplanes from The Great War and the dogfights they used to get themselves into, at old-school, old world speeds since surpassed in a thousand and one ways and more, as had those old wooden biplanes since been surpassed. As it was though, it was these old school outdated antiquated flying machines I had been dreaming about, if I might not better sum up my dream, just by saying, it was actually flight as a thing and a spirit-releasing, spirit-soaring fact, I was really dreaming about.

Flight, and flying.

As I was often prone to do in my dreams.

The Magic thereof, encapsulated therein, such as this dream. The old school flying machines of yesteryear were just the means by which, upon this night on earth, in my dreams, such as flight was achieved, attained and maintained all par for those old school wooden wings, upon the wings of which, and the woodwork in full of this thing, all of my dreams on this night had walked those wings upon the back of which I was flying.

I was flying, actually flying and it was, at least from my relative point of view at the time, real, albeit a dream, but real regardless, considering everything that happens to you in a dream, happens to you, albeit in a dream.

I really was flying, albeit in a dilapidated, old, chugging, currently in the process of breaking down mid-flight, choking spluttering any old engine-powered Great War biplane, the wings of which in this dream of aces, I'd already earned, for I'd already got me a kill score of half a dozen enemy planes, brought down, taken down, shot out of the sky, hard, for they were the nail's head and I had been the hammer, until I was awoken by such as I took to be the sound of a spitfire eating cloud seemingly just outside of the window, choking and spluttering just as I had been hearing in the dream from my own dream-conjured plane.

A dream I was to come to realize there had indeed been, at least where the new reality I awoke to was concerned, some correlation between my dream, and such as I was awoken by on this night, in itself, the first night, until the last night, between which, and all of the nights and days tallied ever since this one, became filled with dreams the likes of which, it was hard to actually walk the world believing oneself, a man both sane of mind, and actually awake, as opposed to dreaming every single minute thereof it from here on out.

One might say of the fortunes of my fate upon this night on earth, I awoke from one dream and fell headlong straight into another. But as I was awake suddenly, and so too was my brother, the fact that I was indeed still dreaming, failed so entirely to register upon my mind, it never, from this point on, ever actually did. The consequences of which, must surely still resonate to this very day, meaning your day, so many years later as it is now, so many years after the fact as it is, as to place these days, that were such days, consigned now to an antiquity decades old and only getting older with every single elapsed day, Time itself seeks to steep upon that count of the days between your days, and mine.

Another time it must surely seem to you now, an Age removed from thine own world at least, given all that you imagine your world contains and mine did not. For my world is a world that most only lens now through the antiquated old black and white photographs that seem, in some archaic way, to consign these very days themselves, in the minds of later youthfulness, to a black and white past that consisted only of old black and white things.

To the contrary though, given that I was there, and you were not, I can assure you, though you may yourself know it now only in terms of those black and white images of which your mind has had its fill, those of us who were there, lived those days in glorious bright technicolor, and saw nothing in such obvious terms as black, and white.

It awoke me, and I awoke my brother, and together, side by side at the window, we looked out into the night, myself claiming I could still hear it whilst my brother claimed he could hear no such thing: That was when I saw the dragon passing before the face of the moon and I knew my brother had missed this event entirely for he was caught mid-comment upon the very face of the moon itself and his take thereupon just such as that, the face of the full moon, when the dragon crossed it. A black thing, black against the moon's white, and he made no omission to his comments to account for this most fantastical occurrence.

This wasn't the first time, and at the time I was sure it wouldn't be the last time, though as it turned out, it was the very last time that I would ever see a thing that my brother's eyes could not, or didn't want to see, or couldn't see because he didn't believe such things existed to be seen with such as eyes in the first place? As it was, even at the time, I'd already long since given up trying to convince him of the relative tangibility of such as he would have called, nought but my own over-active imaginary fictional things, of which he would say, my days would find themselves filled therewith as if this was in my life, my life's only golden rule, and vocation, to be, and in being, be a dreamer.

As far as I could tell though, on this night on earth, though my brother may very well not have been born with the eyes to see such things as dragons, I had, and I saw it. I saw it because it was there to be seen, I suppose, from a certain point of view I guess.

I just guess or suppose, I suppose, it just depends upon one's eyes, and the relationship between that which one sees, and one knows is there to be seen, betwixt that relationship one's head has with one's heart, for as is known by the wise of such things, as goes one, so goes the other; only, which one is the carrot and which one is the stubborn mule, oft is left for the self to discern, least via some external wit that truly has little insight into thine own, this distinction by thy world, is stamped upon thee instead, like a brand.

Supposing it had all been just another one of my dreams, accounts of which he had stored in his mind, of many and more, my brother went back to bed and thus went back to sleep, but I could not sleep and would not sleep, not again, not on this night and not now for some few nights to come, for I had heard what I had heard, and hoping, *nay*, dreaming that I might hear such things again, I stayed awake and a watch at the window, hoping, wishing, dreaming that I just might see it again, as if, if I just kept up my vigilance, and if I watched the moon without taking my eyes off of it to so much as blink, I just might see it again.

The dragon.

The dragon that had sounded like a stalling plane.

Though there had been two dragons at war the one with the other upon this night, as yet, I had only sighted the one, once, and only heard what I thought was the one plane, just the one time and just as I was waking up and not quite awake, and not entirely at that time, a-dream as it was, but either way, my mind in such a state, both dreaming and awake at precisely the same time, though surely two worlds apart these two worlds of these two minds, what seemed afoot in the one, seemed mirrored by such as, to my mind at least, seemed also afoot in the other, as such, it was no wonder I initially found it impossible to discern which world was which, and what was real and what was not.

The window I went on to place myself at, being our bedroom window, was upon a farm, and overlooked a hundred acres of recently harvested wheat fields, that looked in the moonlight, and the ocean of midnight-blue that was this night on earth, like a painting, for it was perfectly still, and the entire world seemed under the heavy weight of a blanket of such silence, were so much as a field mouse to twitch, out there somewhere, lost amongst a hundred acres of harvested field interspersed with un-gathered hay bales like straw ships upon an ocean of hay, the silence of the world would have been shattered spectacularly. As it was though, the silence endured until suddenly, the disembodied sound of a fighter plane spluttering and stalling and struggling in the sky sounded the night like it was a thing coming down upon the far side of the farm, or not, either way, at this time it was a thing I had no line-of-sight with.

As the window was already open, all I had to do was jump.

It wasn't far.

It didn't strike me as dangerous.

But then again, I wasn't thinking about danger, or that, with this daring midnight escape from my bedroom, I might have been about to place myself in any serious harm's way. After all, to the best of my knowledge, and the constant reminders I was oft to receive in passing from both my mother, and my brother when he actually begrudged me such things, I had, from the moment I was born, at least up until this moment, lived what might be best described, as a charmed life.

Mother's little good luck child, my mother used to call me.

My brother called me, other things, and less flattering things than that.

Fortunately, there was fresh hay beneath this window I jumped from at the back of the farm before the meadows started their rolling sprawl from here on out and all the way to the horizon and back again, with just one or two trees standing like arboreal islands amidst a sea of freshly cut straw out there casting strange shadows upon account of the night. It was upon this fresh hay I landed, in my pyjamas, barefoot and brisk as I gathered my wits and raced out across the grass before the fields began true. I actually ran backwards, keenly looking up and over the rooftop of the farm within which my brother and my aunt and my uncle and other assorted youthful farmhands, brought in all par for the war effort to lend my uncle a hand upon the farm with this year's much anticipated harvest, as all of his sons, actually my cousins, in being of the right, if not ripe, age, had all enlisted in the war and been sent away.

Though I could hear it, I couldn't see it and saw nothing of this thing until I tripped over something and hit the ground, landing flat upon by back and thus was caught looking straight up when the underbelly of the dragon soared through the night sky directly above me. A thing on fire this thing as it seemed to me, burning with the most unusual flames I'd ever seen in my life before now. I scrambled to get to my knees and then to my feet, by which time, as best as I could tell, the dragon must surely have actually come down in one of my uncle's fields.

I ran, once I'd picked myself up, and gathered my wits, I ran, for I wasn't thinking. Again I'd seen a dragon, a thought-fantastical mythical Magical beast and one the world only entertained the existence thereof betwixt the covers of children's books and fairy tales and fantasies that often boldly claim the true lore and legend of their brooding beasts. But I'd seen what I'd seen and I already knew what it was that I'd seen, was a dragon. Such as I thought in my madness, and this dream delirium, was a flesh and blood and bones and stones and all, real world bona fide dragon.

And you may very well say, sense had escaped me, but it thundered upon impact with that field it half-crashed, and half managed to land upon somewhat successfully given the sheer struggle of a glide pre-landing, pre-crash, it had been locked in a deadly battle of wits therewith; to crash and burn or not to crash and burn, that at least had been this thing's only consideration as it came in low, an impact with the ground already inevitable at this point.

The second dragon simply fell out of the sky, straight down, and impacted into the same field as the first, only removed the one from the other, where their final resting places were concerned, by a few acres or so of hay. Having cleared the garden and the hedge, and entered the fields, I ran, cherishing the moonlight for that and nought but that alone afforded me, even at a distance, sight of the dragon, that even on the ground now, and even in the full moonlight now, looked a black beast indeed.

Like a plane that had actually landed, this black dragon seemed upon my initial sighting of it upon the ground. So much so, I almost took it to be a plane, and a German fighter plane at that, one that was *that* one second, and a dragon the next, if it wasn't precisely both of these things simultaneously at precisely the same time as it seemed to me as I raced towards it?

In being both a plane and a dragon, a rigid mechanical machine of a thing seemed this black dragon, the shape of which, that afforded the plane the form of such as a dragon, seemed in a state of transfiguration I thought as I approached it, myself as yet with distance enough to see this thing in full from afar.

I stopped when my wits could take it no more, and I felt

like I had to stop, least I get so close to this beast, about which I knew nothing, some harm's way on my part might actually come of encountering up close and personal, this dark but magnificent creature, be it such as that, a creature and not so obviously anything but just such as that, a dragon? So it was, I was stationary when I saw the one so obviously parted the one from the other; the German fighter plane, for it was a German fighter plane, took upon the shape and form and function of precisely that, a mundane real-world plane, whereas the dragon for its part in this act of separation, seemed to shy away from this thing's steel, retracting its wings and seeming to diminish in size as a single pilot, for the plane was such, it only sported a single pilot, a German Ace no doubt, removed himself from the cockpit and fell, obviously a wounded man, from the plane's fuselage, down onto the cut straw of the field beneath him.

He fell enveloped in the guise of a dragon.

I saw this plain and true.

He was both man, *and* dragon.

A flesh and blood and bones and stones man, whereas the dragon was of a noticeably immaterial ethereal nature, such as sported the form of a dragon, in a size that bore some relationship to such as was at its core at this time, which in this instance was a man, having previously stretched itself to better resemble the actual fighter plane itself, least it had been the actual fighter plane that had literally, and figuratively, stretched itself to better emulate the form, and because of it, the function, of a dragon?

A **Black Dragon**.

A **German** dragon.

A *STRICT DISCIPLINARIAN BEAST* born of nought but a **German** nightmare.

A **fantastic Magic** this thing!

A **fantastic Magic** darkly.

Out of black light flames and night this thing seemed made. A burning thing I took it to be, and writhing and snapping at the very air out of which this thing seemed to take its form, so might it be, and in being, this thing was dragon: Both beast and beautiful seeing as it was in my eyes that I beheld this thing, that was both an abomination of a preternatural, almost instinctual creature, and beast, that from the look in its eyes, sported no conscience or remorse or pity for the plight of its prey whatsoever; such as would see the world burn if only it could, like it could've, or would've, or should've, had it not been brought down in a spectacular feat of aviation artistry and skill becoming that of a ROYAL AIR FORCE, bona fide AIR ACE.

Though I hadn't seen it, nor heard it much save hearkening to this thing at a distance, there had been in the skies above that bed I had previously laid myself down to sleep upon, deeply, perchance to dream, believing myself for the duration of the night, safe and sound and assured of a night's peaceful servitude to slumber, until so rudely awoken by the sound of a passing aerial dogfight in the dark, for a dogfight in the dark on this night on earth there had been; and though there may very well have been many and more dogfights upon any given night of the week thus far, both near and far most likely seeing as England seemed of late, to be in a state of war, or at least, a state of preparedness for war, this was the first dogfight I was for my part in the war so far, both witness to, and a party thereof, or at least a party thereto, its ultimate and eventful conclusion in my uncle's own fields, upon my uncle's own farm, just behind my uncle's own farmhouse.

An ethereal almost cold-incandescent black fire form of a black fire dragon, afforded its form by its shape though the edges of this thing seemed living flames, albeit black flames that seemed ill-provisioned to have the combustible guile or gall to so much as scorch the ground this man came to find himself struggling upon. A man on fire without true flame he seemed, writhing and hard-pressed by torments I couldn't see to save him from, and all around him, the ethereal form of a dragon sat like a shroud, like he was wearing this dragon like a jacket, like he'd worn his fighter plane, as if it was a thing he'd actually strapped on, so too seemed now, the dragon he was wearing.

When he suddenly raged, so too did the dragon.

He managed to stand and as he did so, so too did the dragon rise, a trick of the light this thing, like a mirage at the centre of which, was a man. He flourished for wielding, combat-ineffectively, for I took him to be sporting this thing like it was a weapon of some kind, something strange in his hand, such as seemed to me a length of slender wood he did not know himself was broken mid-shaft, presumably upon account of that crude black oil his aviation goggles, still affixed over his eyes, were dripping in.

When some force expelled this broken shaft of a wooden thing from his hand, a force I could not suppose as is, the origins thereof, he drew instead a Luger from his holster, and began shooting at ghosts as it seemed to me as I just stood there, frozen, transfixed, unable to move or make a sound, not even when he turned to face me, suddenly seeming to notice me, or sense me perhaps, for he aimed, and seemed about to shoot straight at me, a killing shot, when suddenly the scarecrow only twice as far from this man as myself, turned on a sudden whim of the wind upon its off-axis strut, creaking like a thing cawing as it did so, thus redirecting my assailant's shot away from me, at the expense of a little of this scarecrow's stuffing, for 'twas shot twice in the chest I think, given I saw two impact holes in the old shirt it was wearing and two exit wounds shedding straw for a few feet in the wake of these two powerful bullets that sped off into the night to do no more harm down on the farm than this.

Holding the Luger with one hand, and gripping suddenly his face with his other, trying to clear his aviation goggles of oil but only smearing the oil he was dripping in, with the palm of his burning glove, the flames from which leapt from this glove, onto his face before they spread, over his head and down his back and all the way to his heels, both legs, leaving him nought but the black shape of the shadow of the shape of a man breathed in flame, just seconds away from combusting into the veritable inferno he became. The oil from the engine that had ruptured mid-air, acting now where the flames were concerned,

17

as an accelerant.

Still he raged, screaming German expletives most likely from the sound of him, until finally one of several wild shots loosed from the sidelines put a bullet in this thing's head, and down fell the man, bringing down a dissipating dragon with him at the same time, until there was just a man, a smoking smoldering man, a German fighter pilot burnt and blackened just lying there upon the shattered hay.

Only when the summer's sunbaked hay combusted, did I react, for these flames swept across the hay swiftly, drawing my attention suddenly to a wrecked Spitfire, smashed almost unrecognizably an acre and a half away. It was from this crash that the Royal Air Force pilot had walked away alive, most likely sporting some few bleeding scratches upon him until the German pilot just so happened to catch him with a random potshot and shot this already-staggering man down only for him to get back onto his feet long enough to repay the favor.

Fortunately, much to the fortunes of my coming fate, I found this man alive, albeit wounded, and on top of this he seemed to have already taken much hurt upon this night on earth, but all that seemed to pale in comparison to the simple fact that his actual walking away from his absolutely-annihilated upon impact, Spitfire, was a bona fide miracle. 'Do you see me boy?' he asked, still at this time lucid enough to be in a position to ask me questions, for he actually asked me twice as it was. 'Do you see me boy?' he said again.

'Yes sir,' I said to him. 'Of course I see you sir. I'm not

blind sir.'

'Raven Mocker,' he said to me, these his first words upon realising I was kneeling beside him suddenly, my back to those sweeping flames I did not know had already reached the farmhouse.

'Raven what?' I asked him as he lay there, sprawling and damn near insensibly delirious. A man of about thirty-five or thirty-six years of age, and old therefore for a Spitfire pilot given I seemed to remember some article in the newspaper that made the claim the average age of a fighter pilot was just nineteen. No doubt, I'd always suspected, due to some correlation between actually being a fighter pilot, and actually being old enough to have some sense of one's own mortality, and that worth one ought to imbue the life of another therewith, as thee would have said other, see thee, likewise. War naturally being thus, a young man's game, no doubt designed to rid the world of wise old men.

'Skysong!' he said, his eyes rolling. A man from the sound of him, given his King's English, and the look of him, he seemed an officer and a gentleman this Royal Air Force fighter pilot. Such as one might call, least he be afforded the opportunity to say it of himself first, a very splendid chap indeed.

'Skysong?' I questioned. 'What means Skysong? I don't understand sir. I've never heard of this thing before, whatever it is.'

'Skysong,' he said again. 'You must get me back to RAF Skysong.'

'RAF Skysong?'

'Do you hear me lad!'

'Is that some kind of a base? An airfield perhaps sir?' I asked him, hoping I might gleam from him some better sense of his dire predicament before he passed out, which, though I was no field medic, nor well versed in much first aid beyond earning that very badge at cub scouts many years earlier, he seemed most likely to do.

'Skysong!' he said, his voice still strong at this point, though the look in his eyes was saying to me, other things. 'Fate of The Nation boy!'

'Our Nation?' I found myself asking. 'England sir?'

'Fate of The Nation,' he said, and that said, he passed out, but was not dead. I know. I checked to be sure, after all, this man had saved my life so I had to be sure, that, if there was anything I could do, or via omission of action not do, to save this man's life, I would both do it, or not do it, regardless. Either way, I was going to save him, after all, it seemed to me, this chap, like the other chap, both of whom it seemed had fallen straight out of my dream, had seemingly done just that as it was, they'd fallen out of my dream.

Two fighter pilot Air Aces, soldiers first and foremost it seemed, both of whom had-had at the other, and vice versa in a battle of wits and dogfight until rendered unto such as the cat dragged home they found themselves, ending it all with a ruddy-muddy *pistols at dawn* gunfight upon an English meadow, the one facing off against the other, and vice versa, both trying to make some allowance or compensation for their aim gone askew; the German upon account of that burning black oil in his eyes, and the Englishman upon account of that blood in his, both of whom seemed to be loosing bullets the one at the other wildly, sending shots zipping off into the night, here, there, and everywhere they both aimed their pistols, and actually fired more bullets than surely such as the pistols they possessed could possibly have held.

It was like nothing I'd ever seen before.

Not even in my dreams did I ever dream of such as this.

All par for this confrontation upon the ground, one of them was shot dead, and the second of them, the Englishman, was just shot. Hopefully just wounded with a wound that wouldn't, all being well, prove mortal for this fine and dandy sporting chap who'd come to my aid at a time of dire need. After all, the German fellow seemed to be about to shoot me dead, which in my eyes, didn't seem all that sporting seeing as it was this fellow I'd seen go down, and therefore it was this fellow I raced out of the farmhouse to save in the first place.

Ruddy-muddy German!

He'd been one of them strict disciplinarian types from the look of him, like the ones I'd seen in a cine-reel portrayed as the real villains of this Europe-wide theatre of German madness, and that German fighter plane he'd crashed in, didn't look to be the usual run of the mill German fighter plane. At least, it was none of the fighters I was for my part familiar with upon account of whatever accounts of these things had been made in the newspapers of late or the newsreels of the local cinema. It was neither a **Messerschmitt**, the BF-109 or the BF-11, or a **Dornier** or a **Heinkel** or **Junker** or **Stuka**, but something else.

Something different. Something brand new perhaps, and hopefully by this Englishman shot down upon its maiden test flight such as had, as surely as it was here, a thing crashed upon an English field, brought it over England to take its chances upon a night such as this one, so might it try its luck out in England's skies. As it was, its luck had failed it completely, and *his luck* failed *him entirely*. Certainly it was of a like kind, the German plane, but different, and besides, it had been for the most part, painted jet-black but for silver insignia.

It had also been a dragon this thing.

This German fighter plane had actually been a dragon, right up until the moment this plane was parted from its pilot, by the efforts of the pilot himself, shot down as he had been, upon such fields as would seem unto his wits, foreign soil, and to me, just the green-green fields of home.

The Englishman on the other hand, he seemed to have made landfall in a Supermarine Spitfire from the look of the bird he'd not so much landed, as crashed, insomuch as, he just seemed to fall straight out of the sky, the plane he was wearing and the dragon camouflage that said plane was wearing, and all, as if this thing, this spectral form it had been wearing like a bodysuit, a lead dragon.

I stood up and away, shocked, but not as shocked as I was

when I turned around, and realised even then, for everyone in the farmhouse, it was already too late.

Come dawn, and the cold cruel light thereof, all was ashes and embers, the farmhouse was lost, and all of the fields were ablaze for as far as my eyes could see. And those dragons, of which there seemed in the haze of the flames, many and more, trying desperately to put out the flames with furious geyser-like eruptions from their throats, not of flame for what would have been the good in that, but water: For they were water dragons these things I saw as the whole world burned down around myself and the unconscious ROYAL AIR FORCE ace lying insensible at my feet, a wall of flames around us, behind which, and from midnight until dawn and the first light thereof, the water dragons labored to douse the whole world if they could, or could've, or would've, or should've, if only these water dragons had been able.

2

RAF

SKYSONG

A natural cleft in the field with a shallow natural brook at its center, saved our souls for those some few hours we sheltered there from the storm of flames that had swept the whole world as it seemed to my eyes into a raging inferno. Ourselves, meaning myself and the man I was dragging, did not re-emerge from the cleft in the field until it was dawn and the world was scorched embers everywhere, and mist. Not a morning mist steeped in the delights of dew, but a smoke, stretched thinly into wisps and world interspersed with the embers thereof. Over scorched straw I dragged him, making the road by daylight and morning to realize those things I thought water dragons were naught but the green Betties the farm had been lent by the army, being used by the army to fight the flames.

I had forgotten about the soldiers stationed in the local village, and their small camp in fields that were not my uncle's but belonged to a neighboring farm entirely. Between that farm and my uncle's farm, there had stood a natural border of hedgerow, but I don't suppose where the flames were concerned, they cared to make the distinction where one farm was concerned and the other. As it was, for the most part, the soldiers had fought the fire upon their own lands to save both their camp, the farm, and probably the village as well, only getting the fire pushed back in time to be entirely too late to save my uncle's farm and all who had been asleep within it.

All was scorched earth and smoke and embers.

Once I had dragged him all the way to the road, I stopped, mostly to catch my breath and to take a moment to discern just what it was I could see further down the road, lost to my eyes upon account of the smoke drifting across the road in full, like a fog, sweeping with that breeze that swept this cloudy surf from one field, across the road entirely, and across those scorched sands once hayfields of plenty and bountiful mirth and more, all gone now, all lost to the storm of flames that seemed in their dance to have lead the entire world to burn last night.

I thought I saw my brother's ghost in this smoke, and I know I found myself spontaneously calling out to him before such things as tricks of the mind and wisps of world that remind one of other things had gripped me so, damn near blindsiding me from those other duties currently mine to see through to whatever ends. Having called out to this herald of woes, and hearkened for a response from this trick of my mind, I heard from my brother's ghost, not a sound, for he was not there, and such as I had only thought I'd seen, I merely took to be a mirage, a shimmering haze of fine smoky mist within my mind, that had painted in a picture of my brother, wandering, lost and destitute but this was perhaps naught but wishful thinking upon my part.

Out of this mist walked a single horse, drawing a single sat alone man upon a single cart, whose going was slow and labored and somber I thought, both horse and man and cart too if I was being honest with myself, for all seemed to sport an air of maudlin and melancholy with not a sense of Malachi about them at all, which is to say, jest.

It was because there were bodies, burnt and black and still smoking in the back of the cart, and though I thought he would surely stop at the roadside right where I was stood, he did not. He did not stop where I stood with a wounded Royal Air Force pilot at my feet, an obviously dragged man, as was I obviously the one who had dragged him, the difference in stature between myself and my burden, great and great enough to have made my dragging this man an endurance I had not the heart in me to renege upon, given I felt like, just upon chance act of hearing him out the night previous, I had in some way promised this man I would not let him down.

Perhaps that, and that alone had afforded him with the

peace of mind to let himself sleep, albeit, pass out on me, his story only half told, and perhaps for that, and that alone, this man's story in full, did I persevere so as to see it done. And I had. I'd seen him to the roadside and it was here, at the roadside, that truly all of my troubles were begun.

The man on the cart seemed not to see me, and I had not the wits or the words with which to draw to myself the much-required attention I needed, so I just let this fellow pass me by. There were soldiers marching down the road, about twenty soot-stained blackened soldiers who looked dead on their feet having fought the flames and the inferno all night long, only walking away now, like ghosts drifting within the smoke. They too just marched right past me without a word or so much as a look in my direction as I stood there, too exhausted myself to burden these men with such as seemed to me a burden beyond their cares for such as further burdens.

There was a second horse and cart, rider-less and runaway but for its ambling pace, this horse simply following the first horse and cart perhaps? Seeing it emerging from the mist as the soldiers passed me by, I waited and sure enough, I found myself leaving the side of the road for the road's center so as to stop this horse and requisition its cart to my own ends and my hurt man's sole purpose for being at my side, which was so might I see this wounded man to Skysong, whatever that was, whatever Skysong would prove to be.

RAF Skysong.

It sounded to me like an airfield most likely.

Seeing him onto the back of the cart wasn't easy but once I'd got him over one of my shoulders, I managed to resituate him onto the cart's back upon a shallow bed of straw, before I placed myself upon this cart's driver's bench. But first I found myself retrieving from the ground something my wounded man had dropped, insomuch as this thing I picked up had fallen from my wounded man as opposed to actually having been dropped by him. It must have fallen out of his bomber jacket most likely, be this thing previously a thing the wounded man had stuffed into said bomber jacket?

Naturally I had no idea what it was, but it was wooden and in length seemed slightly more than a foot long, and rather like some part of the Spitfire and in that sense, some gear lever or throttle perhaps but be this thing such as that, it was a strange thing that only barely sported a resemblance to such instrumentation, be it even anything of the sort? Evidently it had caught a bullet, thus leading me to discover the wounded man's injury was from a rather nasty splinter seeing as this wooden thing still sported the bullet it had stopped from killing my wounded man dead. Least this thing had merely stopped a first or second bullet depending upon the order of things? Certainly my wounded man was still out for the count of the night entirely and this morning in full so far, but at least his heart was still beating. I know because I checked. I had to check, for there didn't seem to me much point in making much haste over a corpse.

But he proved still alive, only unconscious and not from

loss of blood for I had for my part quite successfully addressed the issue of his bleeding over the course of the evening having utilized this man's own silk scarf as both a dressing aid and a tourniquet. There was little else I could do for him, if anything else at all, save see him safely to a doctor or next best thing, short of the next best thing for him turning out to be at the end of this ordeal, an undertaker or at the very least, a mortician.

I thought the thing I'd retrieved from the ground, upon a little closer inspection the broken end of a gentleman's walking stick perhaps, for it was capped at one end with an elegant golden crown shaped like a shire rose I supposed, and obviously Tudor in its affinities but not affiliations. The tapered end of this length of wood was broken and splintered so I truly had no real idea of just how long this thing had originally been, myself unaware at this time that barely an inch or so of this piece of wood was missing.

I saw it sported wording, from which I read plain and true enough-

IN THE NAME OF THE KING

&

BY ROYAL DECREE & APPOINTMENT TO THE KING

Curious words for a throttle leaver I thought.

And a curious thing for my wounded man to have salvaged from the wreck of his downed Spitfire, short of his every act and endeavor first and foremost, having made landfall upon a sizeable square-baled and square-stacked large cube of hay. One he'd annihilated entirely with all the destructive force of one Spitfire fallen from its purchase upon the very air of the sky itself.

I kept this thing whatever this thing was because he'd kept it, and besides, most likely it had actually saved his life by some stroke of good fate and splendid fortunes upon his part. Thus having afforded my wounded man a little bought luck, paid forwards upon his fortunate stowing of this thing within his jacket, I hoped it might thus afford me a little luck too. Supposing this thing's luck, a blanket field, I set it upon the cart beside him where it would sit safely, our going sure to be so slow this thing would not be shaken free of the back of the cart.

A thing that denoted rank or maybe even regiment I thought it, for I did not easily allow this thing to slip half as easily from my mind as it perhaps ought to have, but that said, with a hundred and one other considerations vexing the very spirit of me as is, I didn't let such as this abstract out of place artefact blindside me entirely. The day to face, and a wounded man to see better situated and secured than he presently was, lying as he was, bloodied upon a little straw and as good as dead to the world albeit still a man with a pulse.

I felt I owed this officer and a gentleman a duty.

A duty to the man first and foremost, and to my Country second and surely The King of England third, for he was not here and I was, and none but I would see this wounded man safe if at all he was to make it alive and to safety. Safe as he was, and safe as he seemed, there lingered always the threat of mortal danger should he finally succumb to wounds I had perhaps for my part, played down the act and parts thereof the play these wounds had thus caused the boards of this man's theatre to darken so.

Certainly there seemed a shadow over this man's face, but I did not take it to be death. Death for this man's spirit and soul could wait I thought, and be kept waiting at least until such a time as my ward and thus this burden of a sort, be handed into the apt and able hands of some other soul better suited and situated, if not just better equipped to better diagnose or address all of this man's present cutting edge of Time, worldly ills and ailments.

And that was that, I never saw my uncle's farm lands again, the farmhouse of which, that had stood some few hundred years most likely, having been razed to naught but embers now was naught but a patch, black against black, smoldering amidst a landscape of scorched earth and idle empty green Betties.

My back to my uncle's farm, I sat there, seemingly a prisoner or slave to the horse's own pace as it simply plodded on, its hooves clipping and clopping against the old road as we made our way, at the back of the somber procession of death wagon and marching men following said death wagon as I was following them. A few miles of road later, we reached the outskirts of the village where some mobile military activity was afoot, for I saw a jeep and a couple of military MPs loitering outside a single standalone building upon the outskirts of the village that the army had requisitioned for their own purposes. It seemed a checkpoint of sorts, and these soldiers seemed stationed so as to be a guard of a sort, inspecting all traffic upon the road both leaving the village and entering it.

The first cart, upon which some seven or eight scorched bodies lay dead and charred, and still smoking, had been abandoned just before the red and white striped barrier that barred for blocking the road beside a single standalone pillbox of a guard's lean-to. Behind this, there was a large anti-aircraft gun surrounded by a raised wall of sandbags tall enough to conceal the base of the gun but not its barrels.

My brother had wanted to be a gunner.

He'd have appreciated the anti-aircraft gun more than I, for I was more of an aircraft man myself.

As it was, at least in my head, but not yet my heart, I already knew I'd never see my brother in the living flesh again, given I felt sure I would come upon that cart upon which his dead body lay, once more; it seemed inevitable of the road I'd decided to follow, not to mention, said cart in the first place.

I stopped a few horse's lengths behind the first wagon, and watched a moment the soldiers marching on down the road beyond the barrier, a half mile of road left to them before the village, the next standalone building of which was the village pub: The Horse & Hob.

Dismounting from the cart, I approached the guard station only to be detoured by the crossing guard who left his pillbox to intercept me, but only when I was a good ten feet from the cart, for prior to this, he didn't seem to see me at all, and not at all even, given the look that suddenly came over his previously complacent expression. 'Now where the ruddy-muddy hell did you just appear from lad?' he asked me once close enough to me to do so without having to raise his voice over the otherwise silence of this crossroads.

'That cart,' I said.

'This cart here that I just watched walking this way with seemingly not a soul on-board?'

'You mistake yourself soldier,' I said. 'I was behind the horse the whole distance. Perhaps the sun was in your eyes?'

'Well aye as maybe. Well I see you now lad.'

'As I see you soldier.'

'That's lance corporal that is to you boy.'

'As you say,' I said to that.

'What's your business here lad?' he asked me, his guard down, his rifle against his back, the flap upon his holster buttoned. Like a regular Somme Tommy he looked to my eyes, from his boots to his green helmet, the chinstrap of which wasn't fastened but loose beside his either cheek.

'Please sir,' I said to him. 'I have a wounded man. He needs help.'

'Wounded man you say?'

'Yes sir. A pilot sir. RAF sir. He crashed last night upon my uncle's farm. Caused the fire sir.'

'A pilot you say? Caused the fire you say?'

'Wounded sir. Insensible sir.'

'Well seems to me lad, your wounded man has walked away.'

'Walked away?'

'Well he ain't here now is he lad,' said the soldier who had walked close enough to my cart to be able to see upon its side-less flatbed back, just that loose straw that lay there, with my wounded man upon it.

'What do you mean?' I asked.

The soldier gestured to my cart. 'Where is he then?'

I looked at my wounded man, and then back at the crossing guard and realized, though I couldn't understand why at this time, that the one soldier couldn't see the other. My wounded man was not there to be seen in the soldier's eyes though I could see him plain and true, still lying insensible upon the straw. 'You think he just walked away?'

'Maybe he wasn't as wounded as you thought lad. And you say he crashed upon your uncle's farm?'

'His Spitfire sits in pieces upon one of my uncle's fields. There's a German plane too, and a dead German pilot. They fought sir. In the sky and then upon the ground with their pistols drawn. They shot each other.'

'I think you're pulling my leg aren't you lad?' he said to me.

'No sir. Never sir.'

'Spitfire you say? German plane you say?'

'Yes sir.'

'In these skies just last night you say?'

'German pilot caused the fire he did. He was burning and

set my uncle's hayfield alight.'

'Aye well happens something did,' said the soldier.

'He said he needed to get back to RAF Skysong.'

'Who did?'

'The officer and the gentleman sir,' I told him. 'Raven Mocker he said his name was I think. And he said he needed to be returned to Skysong. Fate of The Nation he said sir. Fate of The Nation.'

'Skysong?' he questioned.

'Yes sir. RAF Skysong sir. Do you know it? Might we not get a message to them?'

'There's no such place lad.'

'No Skysong?'

'Sounds like someone's been pulling your leg lad so you'll end up here pulling mine. Now go on, be off with you. There's dead to be dealt with lad.'

'Yes,' I said to him. 'My aunt and uncle. And my brother too most likely. Claude.'

'You're from Farmer Bird's house?'

'Arthur sir. Arthur Bird.'

'Well lad. Sorry about your aunt and uncle.'

'And my brother sir.'

'Yes well- You all right lad? You got somewhere you can go?'

'Skysong,' I said.

'Well that's a folly lad, you hear me? A folly. There's no such place. And clearly your wounded pilot has hooked it.'

I looked at the wounded man, just lying there in plain sight and wondered why this soldier couldn't see him like I could see him. That was when I remembered what the pilot had said to me, just last night. "Do you see me boy?" he'd asked. What a curious thing to say I thought as his words resurfaced now from the back of my mind to crowd suddenly the very forefront of my mind as I stood there with this soldier who seemed not to possess the eyes to see such as I could see plain and true upon the back of the cart.

'This'll needs be mentioned lad,' the soldier told me, pointing to that standalone stone house surrounded by sand bags, its little square windows sporting white tape like kisses upon each pane of glass. 'You get yourself inside lad. Cuppa tea is what you need. Kettle will be on I imagine. They'll need radio your story in most likely. What with it being a tale of two Spitfires-'

'Just one sir. Second plane was German.'

'Aye. So you said. And you say there's a German pilot upon your uncle's field?'

'Dead sir. Shot dead and scorched bones now most likely. The fire raged all around us.'

'Us?'

'Myself sir and the wounded RAF pilot. Raven Mocker I think he said his name was.'

'Well that don't sound like any RAF pilot to me lad. Better you get yourself inside lad. Go on. Lads inside will know what to do with you.'

'What to do with me?'

'Aye lad. We'll have you settled upon another farm I suspect. Ow'd man Palmer is it? Few farms down. He's been asking every day for more farmhands. He'll take you in.'

'Take me in?'

'Well can't see you vagrant now can we lad. War on don't you know. All hands are needed. War finds work for everyone. Keeps everyone mobile and necessary does war. Now go on. Get yourself inside. Lads'll get you cleaned up. Probably have some clothes for you.'

'Clothes,' I muttered looking at my soot-blackened hands and only now realizing for remembering I was barefoot and wearing pyjamas.

'Door's open lad. No need to be shy.'

I walked away, leaving the RAF pilot upon the cart having been directed to a door that was indeed open, as in unlocked, and swung open once its catch had been lifted. Inside, the first room had been stripped of all furniture and was discovered to be bare, naught but exposed floorboards and featureless walls. The next room, probably once upon a time, a dining room, but not today, was equally bare but for the backpacks of about a dozen soldiers that sat along the walls.

In this room, there was a large map of the county upon the wall and I was drawn to this, for upon this map was clearly designated all those corners of the county requisitioned by the army for what-not and whatever, there being a war on as it was. I looked for Skysong upon this map, but from this map Skysong seemed amiss, and as best as I could tell, nowhere in the county had been utilized by The Royal Air Force for anything, least, in this being an army map, The RAF positions would naturally be amiss from this thing in the first place?

'Looking for home lad?' said a soldier to me as he walked into this barren dining room from yet another adjoining room.

'No,' I said. 'I know where I am. I was looking for an airfield.'

'Won't see any airfields on that map lad. That's obviously this county that is lad in case you don't even know what county it is you've ended up in, and all of the airfields are all few counties away.'

'You sure sir?'

'Lad needs telling twice does he?'

'No sir. I mean yes sir.'

'Yes sir is it?'

'I mean- Sorry sir- It's just that I thought there might be an airfield close by.'

'What's close by lad?'

'A few counties away you say?'

'Closest airfield's an hour away at least.'

'On foot?'

The soldier laughed. 'On foot you'll still be walking this time next week lad. Now, happens you tell me why you're in the den, barefoot lad in your bedclothes.'

'Farm burnt down,' I said.

'Happens there's not a man alive for fifty miles lad who

ain't aware of that. You were there lad?'

'Arthur sir. Arthur Bird.'

'Bird is it? And weren't that ow'd Farmer Bird's farm that burned down last night?'

'My uncle.'

''Ere, ain't he dead on the wagon outside?'

'Probably,' I said to that.

'And 'ere's you lad, stood 'ere in your bedclothes ain't yer.' The soldier craned for cocking his intention to that doorway he'd stepped through and heckled- 'Sergeant! Sergeant Charmers! You there Sarge?' When no response from this so called Sergeant was forthcoming, the soldier muttered something about me waiting for him and thus the soldier, an artillery man, disappeared into the back room just as passing planes, and the engines thereof sounded in the sky outside.

Suffice to say, I rushed back out to find the crossing guard stood in the middle of the road, his back to me as he covered his gaze from the morning sun and peered aloft into the heights of the sky that on this day was cloudless and a beautiful spotless cerulean blue.

There was a whole Squadron of bombers crossing the sky, heading due east I thought, all lower than their optimal ceiling but not so low these things could be seen any clearer than the ominous black silhouettes in the sky they were. As silhouettes, I knew from the shape of them, that this Squadron of planes consisted of about thirteen Lancaster bombers and a single Vickers Warwick. Even distant, they could be heard, flying in formation with so many planes these things upon such a silent day as this one surely couldn't possibly not be heard, though to hear them was hear only war, such as spoke in naught but volumes of those obvious ever looming deeper, darker troubles ahead, war being war.

If I'd just been a year older, I knew I'd already know more about this war than I currently cared to consider, but as it was, at my age, and being of a reasonable strength and fitness, and what with a farm already being in the family, I guess it made sense to ship my brother and I off to said farm.

I watched, spotting at about the same time as the crossing guard saw it too, a single white dot appear in the sky, obviously against the blue, a descending parachute, upon the tethered end of which, there was suspended a pine crate. Even I was able to gauge it would land a few miles away in distant fields, but as it was, this was not so distant this thing that was coming was not the concern of this crossing guard. He dashed off into the building, blindsiding me entirely as I just stood there, watching him go.

Within a minute as it seemed to my sense of time and the passage of but a minute, I heard a jeep started up upon the far-side of the building and saw a moment later, one army jeep with four soldiers within it, speeding off over the farmland adjacent to the road into the village, in the direction the descending crate would most likely make landfall. I found myself wondering if the crossing guard himself was not also aboard that jeep for even after another minute he was not yet returned to his post.

Supposing I was once more on my own, I approached the crossing barrier and positioned myself behind this thing's counterweight, that I found was easy to push down, thus raising the barrier to afford myself and that cart I thought I would continue my journey thereupon, a clear road into the village. There wasn't a doctor, not since the war swept him away to other duties, but there was I thought, at the very least a vet, if not a nurse perhaps?

The barrier raised, I turned, and was looking back at the cart when such as could-not-but be taken to be a giant Seagull, as big as the Lancaster bombers I'd recently seen in the sky, suddenly swooped down out of the sky, hovering both above and beside the cart, seemingly looking down upon that man still insensible upon it.

It was like nothing I'd ever seen before, this giant Seagull, for like the Spitfire that had been both Spitfire and Dragon, so too was this Seagull both Seagull and something else entirely. A plane, surely a plane that was both plane and Seagull, for to look at this beautiful bird's head was to see behind its eyes, a man. A pilot.

Beating its wings as it hovered there, I watched, and had I blinked I would have missed it snatching up the wounded man in its talons entirely, for so swiftly was this feat or theft accomplished, but a moment later it beat its wings and was away, airborne and soaring south with the RAF pilot cradled in this thing's clawed talons.

Only the trophy he'd kept from his crash remained of him

upon the cart, save a little bloodied straw, and this thing I retrieved hardly realizing that no sooner had I picked it up, I vanished from the world within which, there was naught but the thin air to see me do so, or not, as the case proved to be. Certainly I could still see myself, so the fact that no one else could, as long as I was in possession of Commander Raven Mocker's wand, though I couldn't possibly know it to be anything of the sort at this time, escaped me entirely.

Possessed by a wild driven delight, steeped suddenly with the furious wind of this thing, I raced after the Seagull, my eyes upon the sky and the direction this great bird had taken to, and though had I been thinking more clearly I might not have allowed my impulses to so run away with me, but I was not thinking clearly or so plainly as to even realize I had done what it was that I did. By the time I was speeding down the road heading south, it was already too late. I'd already stolen the idle jeep previously sat upon the roadside and was already bombing it down the road trying not to lose all common and plain sight of the high and mighty giant Seagull that had stolen my ward like he be naught but a chip off of some seaside holidaymaker's fish and chips lunch.

A full thirty minutes I chased it, finding the road and this Seagull's direction complimentary until finally it banked right and I lost all sight of it to trees until I left the road and entered rolling fields, flattening a jeep's width of hedgerow to accomplish this detour. Once upon the meadows, I sped, driving wildly but proficient enough in this task previously mastered with naught but my uncle's tractor to test my aptitude in the driver's seat. The jeep was a lot faster, lighter, and far easier to maneuver wildly therewith, myself soaring over the green-green fields of England as the Seagull soared through the equally picturesque English sky.

When finally the horizon swallowed the Seagull whole, I marked that spot upon the horizon that ate this incredulous thing I was following and flooring the jeep's accelerator pedal, I sped the jeep over the fields and faraway, reaching the point on the horizon just in time to see a new horizon equally swallowing the Seagull. There were hills head of me now, and as there seemed little point in expecting to ever see the Seagull again, I reduced the speed of this chase supposing I'd lost the Seagull anyway.

I was an hour at least making it to the height of the rolling hills up the side of which I'd driven, stopping upon the hill's summit just as an entire Squadron of giant Seagulls soared, white against blue in the heights of the sky ahead of me. And oh, the sheer spectacular exhilaration of sighting in the sky such as this spectacle of Seagulls, flocking as a Squadron perhaps on their way to patrol the skies over whatever stretch of seaside needed such a Squadron as this to protect it.

For what a wonder of the world usually unseen was this flock of Seagulls that were not Seagulls but man and machine in the guise and form of a fully functioning sky-sound sky-worthy Seagull. Aircraft these birds that in being birds were not beastly but beautiful, so serene in the sky and as good as silent in their stealth. Majestic creatures and surely the product of a fantastic Magic indeed, be these sky-sound curiosities Enchanted things of a more Magical ilk?

I found myself with no frame of reference in my world for these wonderful things, but then again, what frame of reference did I think I had for such as dragons and such men as seemed inherently imbued with the ability to conjure such as a shawl of dragon around them, and thus around whatever plane these amazing men in their flying machines had conjured right before my eyes just last night. And as then, so now, for surely I was seeing more or less the exact same precise thing. But these men, these men in their flying machines were not dragons in this instance, but Seagulls.

Giant Seagulls.

Their feathers a beautiful pristine cloud white with sheaths of feathered grey and specks of yellow.

Had I not seen them with my own eyes, I fear even I would scarcely believe such a thing could even exist in the world, but they did, and now that I'd seen such things with my very own eyes, I was left with an insatiable burning curiosity to know, for now I had to know, not least of all for that one incandescent question, that like an itch that would not be scratched by anything less than the answer, and the truth of it at that, wherefore art thou my wounded man?

Raven Mocker he said his name was.

That was a curious name I thought: Raven Mocker.

I did not know for I could not know at the time, that-that

was just this pilot's codename: In case of capture no doubt.

And Skysong, well, that proved to be the greatest wonder of all, and one of the best kept secrets of the war I had stumbled upon thus far. Not that, I was yet to stumble upon this thing called Skysong for Skysong was as yet a good few hours away and as yet still lingering as a thing of intrigue upon the peripheral edge of this day's radar. I did not know for I could not know, that soon enough, almost but not quite seemingly just by chance, would I actually get to know. My eyes as it was, were about to be opened up to a whole new war front, one I quite did not know even existed, given that it was the product of that world behind the world I only thought I knew, that world hidden from the eyes of such as do not have the eyes to see such things, as Skysong; not to mention giant Seagulls soaring over the English countryside in unseen sky Squadrons.

All was curiosity.

All was calm.

The silent serenity of the countryside broken only by the breeze, I shattered it entirely via restarting the jeep's engine only to have it cut out on me and stall a half mile down the far hillside later. Had I really driven that far from my uncle's farm already, as to be out of petrol?

I tried the engine a few times and thus found myself with no choice but to abandon it right where it was that it had died upon the hillside. Supposing I really had no choice but to turn around and make what would have been the long and arduous journey back to that village I barely knew at all, within which I knew not a single living soul but for the village auxiliary postman perhaps, the original postman requisitioned for the war effort I'd always supposed, I was about to take a step back towards the rear of the jeep when a struggling spluttering choking and chugging giant Sparrow careered through the sky almost but not quite directly above my head.

It seemed a thing in distress I thought, this giant Sparrow that was actually a man in a flying machine make believing himself just such a bird as a Sparrow. I watched it gliding a distance before it lost altitude at a staggering rate only to soar up out of its fall from its purchase upon the sky to make a more purposeful run at making a landing upon fields I had for my part, in my position upon the hillside, no clear line-of-sight thereof. So it came to pass, supposing the Sparrow a bird down upon a field only a few miles away, I free-rolled the jeep to the foot of the hill, collided with a hedge, and then a tree, leaving myself to make the last mile on foot, and barefoot at that, still wearing naught but my soot-stained bedclothes, and a sorry cat-bedraggled world-weary sight I must have been, for surely such as that, surely I was at this time. Certainly I would not myself have doubted that much at least.

It was not until I had cleared a small hill, and reached this hill's shallow summit that I came to realize the Sparrow hadn't so much as crashed into any old choice field, but had in fact made an emergency landing upon a field clearly designated by the war effort as a landing strip of runway field. And there it was, a modest airbase of some few hangers and several miles of field-flattened runway upon which, but for the Sparrow, not a single plane was sat. But I could see, even from a mile or so away, it was clearly an RAF airbase and countryside airfield I was looking upon from this distance. Against all expectations, I just knew this strange airbase had to be it. This had to be RAF Skysong, for there was Magic on the air, that seemed so rife with this static Sorcery, and given that Magic knows Magic, despite myself not having been introduced to this one inalienable fact as yet, I just knew I'd found it.

For there it was, right in-front of my eyes.

And what a sight for soaring eyes alive it was: A life-affirming spirit soaring sensation of pure éclaircissement, one that riddled me giddy. For 'tis true what they say, such as I came to learn, just as Magic knows Magic, beauty knows beauty, and oh what a wonderful beautiful sight it was, as English as oak and apples and all seemed to the great sprawling but distant local manor house apart thereof, fields and grounds and all.

RAF SKYSONG itself.

3

THE DRAGONS
COME HOME TO ROOST

I wandered alone, a set adrift cloud upon the ground, blowing in with the winds that bore me on foot to the end of the first great length of grass runway I came to, upon the most extreme northern edge of the airfield. This runway I followed, neat short mown grass between my toes and a gentle breeze cooling yet my smarting singed skin. Another scorching hot mid-summer's day this day, as hot as it was yesterday but unlike my uncle's fields that had been reduced onto all but dry straw, the green Betties having barely afforded a few square acres of scorch any refreshment at all or reprieve from this dry hot summer, the grass beneath my feet seemed lush and fragrant and not dry at all.

It was almost like, upon account of this distinction I have made, like leaving one world behind so might I step so entirely into another, my original world became itself naught but a dream given this brand new reality opening up in-front of my very eyes. And I knew I was seeing something almost but not quite, otherworldly, for otherworldly this world was not, save in making any distinction at all between this world and that world it served entirely in secret, otherworldly it made said aforementioned world seem suddenly in my mind. I could feel it in my stones and bones as my father used to say of the human body, bones and stones and all. And I could feel it between my toes, for this green-green grass I was treading, like no other grass I'd ever trodden upon before in my life, never felt more like the green-green grass of home.

This was England.

This was home. This was where the heart was. I could feel it, sense it and damn near taste it at the back of my mouth, like a thought for a feeling that came to balance itself upon the very tip of my tongue, and anywhere but at the very forefront of my mind. As yet it seemed but a secret whisper, speaking of sweet nothings and secrets most don't have the ears to hear let alone the eyes with which to see. What might a more mundane minded soul have seen here on this day I honestly cannot say, for I saw it all plain enough, for to me, and my eyes, such as this airstrip was not an invisible hidden thing.

I walked with no wool over my eyes.

My eyes were open, for my heart was open, not necessarily to the truth but at least open to the search for the possibility of some truth, which came to count for everything. Without doubt

I walked, knowing full well that having set my heart upon the coming hangars these hangars I would actually reach, and these things wouldn't be found to be the curious mirage they seemed at a distance of a mile or so at least, shimmering in this shortening distance with my every purposeful stride, like a trick of the rising heat messing with one's already sunbaked mind.

As it was, I marked in the distance not a single soul, though I couldn't be sure of the greater distance where sat a very splendid grandiose manor house indeed; one evidently requisitioned by The Royal Air Force, as was self-evident I thought of the fact that this manor house's lands, cultivated gardens, fields and all, now served the obvious intention of quite a large airbase. No planes though, grounded or otherwise could I see save to suppose the hangars wouldn't be encountered entirely empty of all things of a decidedly aviation themed free-for-all of eclectic military, albeit Air Force, flotsam detritus.

Upon reaching the inner end of the runway, I found myself mesmerized by regimented windsocks all marking the direction of the wind, and then this wind's change as all of these things, like soldiers on drill mid-inspection, alternated in unison and collective orchestrated accord, all par for this dance of uniformity and singularly minded beast, turning from a south-southeast direction to due east right before my eyes.

I walked on, enchanted.

So blue the near cloudless sky and those clouds there were, distant and white, only added to the beauty of this day's scorch for the sun was high, all par for its midday climb across the rolling heights. Against this blue, I saw the greenest trees I'd ever seen in my life, and here and there, wherever these trees cast their shade, there sat plain dark canvass deckchairs, a few dozen at least, but there seemed to my sense of sight, and my preternatural sense of the stillness of the world, there truly seemed no one around to fill these seemingly forgotten about things.

No anti-aircraft guns I noticed, not anywhere to be seen and seemingly no sandbags at all, which seemed a first for me for as long as I cared to remember these days. This was war, and war and sandbags, at least to my mind, had thus far walked hand-in-hand, if not just side by side for the entire stretch of the distance thus far. Upon reaching the open door of the first hangar I reached, I looked in upon no planes at all, but such as I took to be all the tools of the trade of whatever loitering ground crew was usually to be found haunting such things as aviation hangars. But today, there were none.

Hearing a crackling whistling wireless music suddenly, coming from a hangar a few empty hangars away, and so obviously a wireless broadcasting English free radio, Glenn Miller, my brother's favorite song, I followed my ears to the source of this song and found it was indeed a wireless radio, and not a military field radio as I'd been expecting but such as would be found in almost every home in England, polished walnut the veneer of this fine thing. There was no one here either, and strangely, the radio seemed to be tuning itself seemingly of its own accord. Even as I stood there, it changed the station, searching through the static for a perhaps more choice insight into this airfield's war footing. I thought myself hearkening to the eaves this radio was catching in passing of some Squadron of pilots chatting over the cross-waves before more familiar home-spun melodies replaced these choice dispatches overheard but by no means entirely understood. When the wireless died all seemed curiously silent and still once more until the wind changed causing something somewhere to creak ominously.

Restoring myself to the open air, I marked the standalone plane in the distance that I presumed and was right to presume so, had previously been the Sparrow, but where now the pilot who had conjured this illusion around both himself and that mechanical flying machine of steel and style he had somehow managed to land without crashing, given the hell-for-leather descent whatever pilot had come careering in upon the prayers and wings thereof, such as I had taken to be the makings of a crash landing.

There was though, no crash.

There stood instead, upon a field a half mile away, a Spitfire. A standalone, albeit sitting alone, in a field of its own, lonesome Spitfire. This was it, in itself was a curiosity, for I had seen with my own two eyes, such as the mind behind found it could not thus so easily or obviously deny to my every other sense of the world, a dragon that was both dragon and Spitfire, though truly the dragon façade itself was much more a product of the pilot than it was of the makings of the machine itself. Therefore, some correlation obviously existed between the prowess of the pilot, and that shape of a form of a functioning thing one's plane takes on, be that Seagull, or Sparrow, or Dragon.

That was quite the leap as it seemed to me, from Sparrows to Dragons, all from the same model Spitfire, another Supermarine if I wasn't mistaken. But for the obvious lived-in working feel to this airfield I might have supposed it a ghost town, but whoever had landed the Sparrow, or rather, whatever pilot had actually been the Sparrow had to have been around here somewhere.

I thought the manor house the best place to start and so headed towards this most magnificent stately home given over to what I was to come to learn was RAF Skysong Air Command, airfield and base both, home to the Magical Squadrons of The Royal Air Force and base of operations for all of their sorties and bombing raids. I noticed an idle aircrew at about the same time this first aircrew I was to encounter, and then a second that fell within my line of sight once I'd cleared what was almost the final hangar, these fellows appeared to show no further interest in me than just to stand and stare.

One man, who had been cleaning his dirty oil-stained hands on a rag, continued to clean his hands upon said rag as I walked, giving this fellow a wide enough birth for the two of us to pass at a distance of some twenty feet or so. He said nothing, and did nothing save he watched me simply walking on by. As it was, my tangent towards the manor house great stately front door such, and myself already aligned therewith it, I was certain to pass by other fellows a lot closer than the first.

I did, but these fellows also said and did nothing to either impede my progress or question it perhaps as precisely as they ought otherwise to have done? Both ground crews, six men in overalls to one team, and eight men to the other, all just watched me walking right on by them, all of them seeming to throw in behind me, but keeping a distance of at least ten feet or so where my closest pursuant was concerned and further back for others. All walked behind me, silently, gathering like a flock or a following of sorts, and though I knew them not from the next man, they seemed to afford me this precession's lead.

Until I stopped, and turned around.

They stopped too, seemingly just as curious of me as I was of them.

A moment passed, and then another, and both camps remained silent until a single bold engineer approached me so as to say, curiously enough- 'Sleepwalker or wandering ghost or both from the look of you?'

'Neither sir,' I said to that.

'I ain't no sir lad, happens you don't need to be so formal with us young squire is it?'

'No sir, I mean yes sir. I mean, Arthur Bird sir.'

'Well Arthur,' said the engineer.

'He can see us then?' said another.

'Of course I can see you,' I said to that. 'Be I not so obviously otherwise blind, why would you think me unable to see you?'

'Lad's a Wizard fellas!'

'Well what do you know. And he just happened to wander this way in his pyjamas 'n' all.'

'Perhaps he's walked here in his sleep for a reason?'

'Happens he's been summoned?'

'No,' I said. 'No summons. I followed a Seagull.'

'Seagull is it lad?'

'It snatched my wounded man right out of the back of my cart it did.'

'What's that you say lad?'

'Raven Mocker. My wounded-'

'Commander Raven Mocker you say?' said a man interjecting this point into my point, which because of this comment, I didn't get to finish myself.

'Wing Commander's down as missing,' said another.

'Went out yesterday and didn't come back.'

'Well. Speak up lad. What do you know about it if anything?' I was asked.

'He crashed,' I told them.

'The Commander? Crashed? That doesn't sound like-'

'Ruddy-muddy German shot him down,' I said.

'And that sounds even more far-fetched lad.'

'It did too,' I told them. 'He got the German though. Shot him dead.'

'Shot him dead you say?'

'My uncle's farm. Both planes came down upon one of my uncle's fields. Both pilots lived. They shot at each other. Both men fell. One dead. One dying.'

'Dying you say lad?'

'I was taking him to get help when a giant Seagull swooped down and bore him away.'

'Aye well Seagull Squadron's airborne today so likely there's some truth to your words lad.'

'And yours?' I questioned.

'What's that you say lad?' he asked me.

'A Wizard you said.'

'Aye and a Wizard you'd have to be to find your way onto this secret airfield lad. Magician at least and a Sorcerer for sure seeing as you can see the Seagulls.'

'And the Sparrow,' I said. 'Followed it here. Thought I was following the Seagull. But I only see the Sparrow?'

'Well if as you say Wing Commander Raven Mocker was wounded, dying even, wouldn't make much sense to bring the man here. Happens he's been taken to the nearest field hospital.'

'Most likely,' I said. 'And I should say, sirs. Last night, I saw both the German dragon, and our good Englishman's dragon I'll have you know good sirs.'

'Lad's a Wizard for sure,' said a man.

'German Dragon?' questioned another. 'What ruddy-muddy German Dragon?'

'It shot your man down,' I told them.

'Like Spell-fire and hymn-stone it did lad! Like Spell-fire and hymn-stone!'

Not an expletive I'd ever heard before, and found myself

questioning it plainly. 'Spell-fire and hymn-stone sir? What on earth does that mean?'

'It means lad. You're a curious young fellow now aren't you? A Wizard that doesn't know that he's a Wizard and he ends up here on a day like this one, at this time. Seems to me young man-'

'Arthur sir. Arthur Bird.'

'Just 'alf a bird lad?' he questioned in jest. 'Where's 'tuther 'alf to yer?'

'Dead,' I said to that.

'What's that you say lad?'

'The German pilot started a fire. My uncle's farm burned down, along with my uncle, and aunt, and my brother, and others.'

"Ere happens that was the cause of the glow on last night's horizon?'

'Most likely,' I said. 'Acres of fields were lost to this fire.'

'Well best you come with me up to the manor house lad. There will be fellows with all kinds of ranks you've never even heard of who'll want to be having a word with you my son.'

'Am I in trouble?'

'Trouble lad? Trouble? Perish the thought sir.'

'Sir?' I questioned.

'Reckon we'll all be calling you sir soon enough if you are that which we already know you must be.'

'Which is what?'

'Why a Wizard of course lad! A Wizard! How's it you've

never realized this before now?'

'What's a Wizard?' I asked.

'Wizards, Magicians, Sorcerers, and folks of an otherwise otherworldly Enchanted ilk as they say just so as to make the distinction, some Wizards being more equal than others as it always seems, as we say, and I just said right here, right now lad. You're going to end up the talk of the entire airbase by evensong tonight you mark my words.'

'Really?'

'Aye lad. It's not every day an undiscovered unsummoned un-enlisted and not-yet-drafted Wizard, just walks onto the runway of the most beyond top secret airfield in all of England.'

'There are Wizards here?' I asked.

'Why everyone's a Wizard here otherwise they wouldn't be here now would they lad?'

'I don't know. To be honest sir, I think you lost me at Sleepwalker or ghost sir?'

'Well, aye and as to that, happens I should have asked you instead, Wizard or Sorcerer lad, or perhaps, from the look of you, somewhere lost in-between is it?'

'In-between a Wizard and a Sorcerer?'

'Can't wait to see what kind of ornithological Totem you've been blessed with lad,' he said earnestly enough and seemingly straight to me before he blindsided me entirely upon account of turning to the other men, most of whom seemed in their forties to me with hardly a young lad or man amongst them, and saying-'We ought to run a book on this one. Sweepstakes and winner takes all. How does ten bob on the nose sound gentleman?'

'You fellows are gentlemen?' I asked.

'Well we might not cut it with the clean cut officers over in their great grand nest over yonder,' he said, cocking his head as an indication he meant when he said, nest, the manor house. 'But standards is standards young lad.'

'Seventeen sir,' I told him just as a jeep pulled up, one of the other grease monkeys of this ground crew in the driver's seat, its engine left running.

'Well seventeen or not, be that true lad or be it whatever, what with our need of pilots and Wizards especially, something tells me lad, you're going to have to earn your wings pretty sharpish.'

'Wings sir?'

'Aye lad! Happens someone somewhere, most likely up at the manor, will more than likely suggest soon enough, once word of you gets around, you be taught how to fly.'

'Fly?'

'Pilot a Spitfire.'

'Really sir? A Spitfire sir? Me sir? Taught to fly sir?'

'Aye and you'll be taught to kill also lad so don't go grandiosing the ruddy-muddy war in your stride. Serious business all this lad. Serious business indeed.'

'Yes, of course.'

'Don't you worry lad. You'll be a scarecrow before you know it and then we'll see won't we. Not asking for a heads up or anything from you lad. Fair's fair. Sweepstakes is sweepstakes.'

'I'm afraid good man, you've lost me entirely.'

'Aye well happens it ain't as entirely as you say, but as to that- You're a Wizard lad! A Wizard! And what with you being here, at this airfield, well that speaks for the birds lad, you've got an ornithological Spirit at the very heart of yer.'

'A bird sir?'

'Aye lad- You're a bird. But just what kind of a bird you'll turn out to be, well, that's what we'll be running our sweepstakes upon. Let's just hope you're not a ruddy-muddy pigeon.'

'Pigeon sir?'

'Pigeon's that last thing we need son.'

'Well here's to hoping I'm a Dragon sir,' I said thinking myself following this man's plot deliberations closely enough to have got the gist of the act going on here, given all seemed a staged theater piece to me. It may very well seem or sound a cliché to thee, so far removed now from these days within which I was at the time, walking through the history thereof, such as those days that were, the greatest days of my entire life, but never in all of my wildest dreams did I ever think I lived in a world I shared with real bones and stones flesh and blood bona fide real world Magicians and Sorcerers and living breathing Wizards.

Be life therefore not a fantasy and a fiction in itself, I honestly couldn't even begin to fathom what otherwise might be true, be such as that, just that, anything but a fantasy and a fiction? Certainly, my world was never to be the same again, ever again, for not a single day in all of the last few months on earth I had to live. For I will, and I'll tell you now, as seems a fit and apt and appropriate time to do so, just so you know, as walked hand in hand with this world behind the hidden veil between the one way of looking at the world, and another way of seeing things far more plainly and clearly entirely, to create such a schism of two ways of seeing the very same one thing, a dream, so too at this time in the world, was the dream thus straddled alongside the very dream of the world, a force attempting to twist all dreamlike things, into a nightmare corruption of function and form and all the beauty inherent therein, all such as this force of corruption was endeavoring to destroy.

I'll put it to you now, as it was put to me, plain and simple and true so might I know, and thus, I tell you now so might you also know, given it might just leave you with cause to alter your perception entirely: There are those who see nothing as a Miracle, and those who see everything as the Miracle that it is: Thus is defined, a Wizard!

Wizards are Miracles of The Magic!

Wizards and Magicians and Sorcerers and Otherworldly folks of an otherwise Enchanted ilk, and thus, in their world, a world hidden in plain sight of such as just weren't born, I thought at the time, with the eyes for such things as Miracles and Magic.

This made me a very fortunate child indeed, and as lucky as my mother always said I was. Stood there soot-blackened and barefoot in my pyjamas, it was like I'd walked straight into a veritable dream come true, and all being well, given all was still well at this time, I might yet be taught how to fly. Maybe even once I'd earned my wings, I'd also earn my very own Spitfire?

What dreams in the sky might come of that?

What nightmares?

What daring and dogfights as we play cat and mouse with the enemy as the enemy tries to play vice versa, pretty much the same game of aces as we. I think, looking back, at the time, this had been my expectation, somewhat rose-tinted and romanticized I must admit now, but in my youth, and truly in possession of naught but fanciful glorified notions of noble air aces fighting it out one on one in a duel of wits and fortunes and one man's fate weighed never so precisely against the fate and fortunes of another man, as when two men are a-sky and athwart sky-ships the one trying to shoot out of the sky the other, and always I thought the best man would win.

I really was that naive.

But then again, I was only just seventeen and knew nothing of the true reality of war, and sky-battle in this Age of Spitfires and Hurricanes and Mosquitos and all manner of mighty manmade flying machine, some of which, dog eat dog single pilot one-man fighters, and others bombers, some five or six or seven or sometimes eight or more souls on-board with little chance of opportunity to bail should anything inevitably perhaps, go wrong, capable of such unthinkable unspeakable horrors all carried out in the name of war.

We were the fire in the sky and we were the fury.

We were the fire in the sky and we were the rain.

We were the fire in the sky and we were the thunder.

All this make-believe and more I had yet to come, for as yet, I was simply sat upfront of that jeep that spirited me away from those aircrews of a handful of hardy good old boys to that manor house I imagined no oil stained rag was allowed within a hundred feet thereof.

'Allow me to introduce to you sir,' the driver said to an obvious officer and a riding-crop wielding gentleman whom was met at the foot of the wide flat stone steps up to that prominent veranda in stone before the tall stately doors into the interior of the manor. 'Arthur Bird. Lad's a Wizard if ever a Wizard there was. Wandered onto the airfield from the north he did. He has word of Wing Commander Raven Mocker sir.'

'Word's already in that man,' said this officer whose name was Willoughby-Chase. 'Man got himself ruddy-muddy shot down didn't he. Bird's a total right off I'm told.'

'Arthur here sir. Happens he saw the whole thing. From the crash to the snatch as it were.'

'Snatch you say?'

'Arthur here says one from Seagull Squadron picked him up and flew off with him.'

'That's need to know only airman and well, sorry old boy but…'

'I don't need to know,' said the driver finishing the officer's sentence for him.

'Quite,' said the officer, such as seemed a stern stickler to such as rules and the King's own at that. 'So- Spellman isn't it?'

'Aye sir, that's just grand sir that is, grand I tells you. Thank you for remembering sir. Much obliged to you sir for that.'

'Well Spellman what do we have here beyond an obvious civilian in his pyjamas?'

'Arthur Bird sir,' I said to him.

'Well Arthur Bird,' he said, gesturing that I should be a thing departed from the jeep. 'I think young man, you'd better be coming with me don't you?'

'Good luck to you lad,' said the driver and that said, and this package of one, me, delivered to the door or as good as, he sped off back to that hangar, where I came to learn, every single man of the aircrews had thrown in for that sweepstake whose sole intention was to discern just what kind of Mythical-Magical fantastical creature of a discernibly Enchanted nature I might just turn out to sport at the very heart of my root soul so to speak, or as would be more apt, my Totem.

'It's not luck you'll be needing lad,' the officer said to me. 'It's your wit about you lad that will best serve you here and in your all and every duty to come lad.'

'Duty sir?'

'Is to England lad!'

'Commander Raven Mocker,' I said. 'He said fate of The Nation to me he did. Just last night when I saved him from the flames.'

'That so lad?'

'Fate of The Nation he said sir. Fate of The Nation.'

'Saved him from the flames did you?'

'He saved me sir, from more and worse sir. Ruddy-muddy German was going to shoot me.'

'A German fellow you say? Where? When?'

'Just last night sir. I saw them both crash. Our man and the German. They were Dragons sir. His was black and ours, well, I guess it sported the look, or at least the markings, and colors, of a Spitfire sir.'

'A German Dragon you say?' he questioned just as shadows passing over us, caused the two of us to both look up into the underbellies of about a dozen Dragons soaring overhead, in formation, having just now returned to roost having completed their most recent mission.

All were Dragons and Spitfires and all were coming in to land, the ground crews active now and able ready willing and waiting to be of some service to this collective airfield's united war effort.

'Well if you can see them,' said the officer. 'You're certainly one of us young man.'

'One of us?' I questioned, yet to take my eyes off of this Squadron of Dragons coming in to land and already landed in the case of one or two Dragons already upon the ground. Truly the spectacle of this was majestic, a magnificent aerial display of flight and form and finesse for all landed as gracefully as a swan a-swim.

One by one they came in to land.

All of them remaining Dragons until the very last of them

to land was landed and there they all were, for one perfect moment of beautiful Magic, a dozen Dragons at least all sat upon a field of their own, some of them actually seeming to beat their wings and stretch both necks and tails as these things twisted and turned and where their heads were concerned, they seemed to snap and bite soundlessly for these things, in being the immaterial ethereal emanations of a visible projection of a mere make-believe imaginary thing, they had neither bite nor bark these Fantastic Magic creatures more construct and thing conjured than an actual flesh and blood and stones and bones creature of a beast, and yet, beastly proportions they possessed until one by one, the Dragons were diminished as the aircrews labored to see each machine safely grounded. The spectacle of a dozen or so Supermarine Spitfires no less diminished by the retracting Dragon-forms that slipped their surly bonds upon metal and machine, so as to be borne by naught but the backs of men, these pilots of these planes who were in being men, and Magicians, both Wizards and Dragons and aces one and all.

4

"WE'RE OFF TO SEE THE WIZARD!"
(OR)
THE BIRD IS THE WORD

'By the way young man,' said the officer, who was actually a Group Captain, to me as we reached the open stately doors into a very stately home indeed, one I suspected was nobodies home now save to say those officers of this Secret Air Command had indeed moved into this manor they'd made their headquarters in full and by no short staffed measure, their home away from home within, after a decidedly military fashion, albeit Air Force; which as best as I could tell, was not just a cut above the usual boots on the ground norm where the army was concerned, but a whole class and a half removed too, where both etiquette and reformed elevated manners and fine grooming were to be observed as said norm as per the rule of this house, technically RAF roost: Where many a brooding Warrior Wizard was nesting as it turned out; from The Magical Marshall of The Royal Magical Air Force, who was at the highest echelon of service in this regard to King & Country, to the lowest Officer Cadet, and then there was me, as it was at this time, even lower than that.

'Yes sir?'

'Welcome to RAF Skysong.'

'Then I've made it sir. Even though my ward did not,' I told him, my inner pride my own, only half diminished in that sheen I had hoped to buff with my delivering of a wounded pilot, back to this airfield he, presumably of late, had been calling a home away from home, least in being such as a pilot, the only true home he knew was up amongst the clouds so high, like a diamond in the sky?

'Your ward you say?'

'Commander Raven Mocker sir,' I said to that. 'He asked me to see him here, but in that, I failed him sir.'

'Well no matter. And that's Wing Commander by the way. Man was a ruddy-muddy fool to be asked to be brought back here what with his injuries I am told. And what the devil was he doing taking a bird out to sky last night in the first place I ask you? I wonder what so possessed him.'

'Yes sir, he was shot sir.'

'By Jerry yes?'

'A German sir. Dragon sir. They got into a shootout in one of my uncle's fields.'

'A shootout you say?'

'A shootout.'

'Seems to me the old boy must have thought himself one of the famed and legendary Wizards of The Old West. Erasmus

Wandslinger himself reborn no doubt.'

'Who sir?'

'You say he shot it out with Jerry yes?'

'A German Dragon sir. Black. It bore silver insignia. Before he lost consciousness sir he told me fate of The Nation lad. Fate of The Nation he said.'

'Talk is over the wireless chatter, he'll live,' said this officer, one whose eyes spoke in silent volumes in terms of that dispatch I received from this officer, though I'm sure he hadn't meant to tell me anything of the top secret sort no doubt. I just found that I knew, and in knowing, though I couldn't be certain how it was I just knew it, but I did. The 𝕲𝖊𝖗𝖒𝖆𝖓 𝕯𝖗𝖆𝖌𝖔𝖓 was both persona non grata, and not to be spoken of openly be thee not this airbase's Magical Marshall talking to this airbase's Air Chief Marshal, or respectively, said Air Chief Marshal talking to the Air Marshal, or he to the Air Vice Marshal, or he to the Air Commodore, or he to the Group Captain, and so on down the ranks, from Group Captain to Wing Commander to Squadron Leader to Flight Lieutenant to Flying Officer to Pilot Officer to Officer Cadet; naturally be whatever information for such ears as theirs. Though I was none of the above, I learned from this officer and a gentleman's eyes, the simple inalienable unquestionable, already-verified but not yet rectified, terrifying truth, was to put it simply, the enemy 𝕯𝖗𝖆𝖌𝖔𝖓 had not shown up upon a single radar station in all of England, Magical, mundane, or otherwise.

Fate of The Nation indeed!

'Good,' I said to that, even though I truly knew not this man from any other stranger encountered all par for our great Nation finding itself at war with another equally great Nation, only one that it turned out, though I couldn't have supposed it at the time as a truth, had succumbed to craven graven raven strict disciplinarian BLACK MAGIC SORCERERS indeed. Dark dire WIZARDS whom, with sleight of hand, and brandished MAGIC wielded unseen behind the Magical seams of the mundane world, conquered the spirit of Germany first, and then used all of the industrial might and backbone and stones of Germany in an attempt to bring the whole of Europe to heel in a single night of military misfortune for millions.

Fortunately, a clearer headed purer-hearted more benevolent Magic fought back and stopped the onslaught of this terror and terrible new reign of un-righteous MAGICIANS, thus bringing their goals of Europe-wide dominance and unquestionable rule, to a standstill and a stalemate, all now being war because of it. All now being all of this because of it. All now being war: A war I had no idea was actually coming here, when it seemed, or at least was felt and thought also, to be a war upon mainland Europe, for mainland Europe, against which, this glorious sceptered isle was holding out, and holding on to the hope, that we might yet be victorious should the war come any closer to our shores than it already had.

Certainly, as it was, and as it was understood by all of us, every single man, woman, and child old enough to comprehend such things across the entire British isles, as goes England, so goes the fate of Europe for a thousand years at least.

DARK REIGN these BLACK MAGICIANS would have.

DARK REIGN and BLACK indeed, should The Light of Europe be extinguished in the world, shy of these BLACK MAGICIANS relighting the fires of the world in their own name, or at least, in the name and image of those, even darker, more dire HIDDEN MASTERS such as even their own hidden hands serve the strings thereof this supernatural preternatural ethereal beast called FEAR.

Be FEAR a beast?

Be it not, an altogether different creature entirely?

All of those pilots, not all of whom were Englishmen, though all had been previously Dragons, approaching the command manor, I was ushered through the great doors and handed over to a young officer cadet a few years my senior and he was told to get me cleaned up. That order saw me washed and given a clean uniform to dress into, such as left me looking only half like a regular soldier and one half something else, something of a decidedly un-militaristic nature and disposition entirely.

I wasn't army nor was I Royal Air Force and the caliber of my upbringing, and my education for that matter, seemed lacking when compared to theirs for the most part, for most men seemed officers and aristocratic gentlemen of varying rank and refined sensibilities, at least, those men who were pilots, or commanders of men who were pilots, and thus up the chain of command, of which as yet, I was not officially apart, myself not even a damned ranker so far removed from the first rung of the ladder that the ladder itself seems a mythical thing hidden by such rarefied heights few damn rankers live long enough to aspire with their reach towards in times of war: If at all, at least officially, I ever was?

Certainly I was clocked upon their radar.

Unlike the enemy Dragon, that wasn't.

The true implications as yet, were yet to be spelled out to me in full and in no short measure of a single punch pulled or blow sent across the bow. I was there. We all were there. From the Air Chief Marshal to me, and all of the miscellaneous ground crewmen in-between. We all were there when The Magical Marshal addressed us all. All guns firing; when it was time to come to it, he came to it ready, willing, and able to keep not a single one of us in the dark of the shade of the German vine for but a second longer.

Fate of The Nation indeed.

All that as yet supposedly behind TOP SECRET doors, closed to the likes of I at this time, I wasn't supposed to know a thing about such things as those things at all, but like I've said, his eyes told me all I needed to know. As soon as I mentioned to him- "Fate of The Nation." I knew, and I knew that he knew, and he perhaps knew that I knew that he knew, but then again, given I read such as that from his eyes anyway, there really had been no need at all and none whatsoever, for this officer to elaborate further.

For now at least, I might as well leave that as a thing that remains to be seen of all that was left of this war. A war that had, though I couldn't possibly know it at the time, hardly even got started yet, given all as yet, was the warming up to the buildup of a battle all the Wing Commanders, and everyone of higher rank than that, from the Air Chief Marshall to the Air Commodore, at this secret airbase saw coming, and all hereafter seemed to serve nothing but the great preparedness of this **TOP SECRET** airbase to be the first inline to combat the coming threat, if not stop it dead in the water, albeit sky, barring such as *THE BEAST* that was coming, not one further inch of sky to call its own. Especially seeing as the sky we would soon enough be fighting and dying for, would be our sky, and not their sky though their sky they had intended to make every single square acre thereof.

The whole world over.

The Battle of Britain as yet a few months away.

For as would go Skysong, so would go the skies over England and The British Isles in full, possibly forever more, if not most likely, forever more and for not a day less for sure.

TRUE STORY- If we'd lost our sky, we'd never have ever been in a position, ever again, to take our sky back from such as had stolen it from us, who no doubt, once they'd stolen our sky from us in full, would equally take from us, our land.

I just happened to be thinking about the sky, just doing up my last few buttons, when I should take a single half-stride in the direction of that tie draped over the back of a chair, that suddenly stripped this room I was in, of its roof just as a single Albatross, a giant, and obviously piloted by a Wizard, or Wizards, for as an Albatross I couldn't discern the true make and model of this beautiful elegant flying machine that seemed unto my every sense of this Magical apparition, more Albatross than steel and glass, and as feathered as those Dragons I'd been witness to the dive and death-throws thereof, at least where the one Dragon was concerned, had been fiery.

I looked up, watched it pass and then noted the sheer absence of roof and therefor any ceiling at all over my head suddenly, and to look now at the walls of the manor was to think this stately home derelict a hundred years and twice as exposed to the elements as that. Why even the walls were rotten and moldy and thoroughly ruined in stately guise and form and elegant decadence, such as surely hadn't known the touch of ought but said elements in a very long time. So said the mold. So said the mildew. And as were the walls rotten, so too were the floorboards suddenly.

There was a hole in the floor now where just a few moments ago I'd actually been standing, and to look down into it, was to see a once great hall below as ruined below as this stately home now was above, and all the way to the exposed skylight where previously had sat a roof, albeit ceiling but now stretched only exposed sky.

I think, it's safe to say, as you can imagine, I was quite taken aback by this curious turn up for the books, for I could not yet know that by taking the half-step I took to reach for something, I quite placed myself outside of that Magical field I had actually previously been well within the field of the force thereof, Wing Commander Raven Mocker's military-grade wand, given I'd been carrying it upon my person this whole time. As it was though, I'd placed it down upon a dresser whilst I'd dressed into those clothes afforded me from the manor house's own provision of such as some otherwise previously engaged quarter master's store of kit and supply.

From this store, my chaperone had helped himself, and though only the boots I was given fit my feet perfectly, as I'd actually been asked my shoe-size where these boots were concerned, everything else seemed, size-wise, a bit hit and miss really: But as it wasn't much more than socks, trousers, and a shirt, these things, even though they weren't the perfect fit, would have to do, seeing as my only other alternative would have been to join the war against the German *STRICT DISCIPLINARIAN DEVILS*, as it was, in my pyjamas.

Certainly The Royal Air Force had standards.

Not strict disciplinarian standards, by German standards, but standards all the same.

After all, this was England.

And all for the King, George VI, England would remain England, home of the free and the home of the brave, that place where everyone's home is a castle, be it made out of sticks and stones, straw or mud; England being England: Such as was already, ready, willing, able, and keen at this time, to give the ruddy-muddy German a run for his money, given it seemed the German, despite his costly war reparations from The Great War, and that debt he already owed the world, actually must have had money to burn, burning holes in his pockets, albeit American money, but money nevertheless; given we know now that which we didn't know then, that it was an **AMERICAN EVIL** feeding the **GERMAN EVIL** its own due, seeing as this **EVIL** we fought, in being **THE EVIL** we fought, had no country of its own, until it invaded Germany first, and then tried to take on the world, in no small measure given that measure of the world this **EVIL** with this **WAR** was making a play for in full.

From where I was stood, and given the sheer state of disrepair the manor house was in suddenly, I could see through great gaping gashes in the walls, able to see through holes via holes via holes, that it wasn't just the manor house in ruins, but all of its grounds too, from its cultivated gardens and lawns to that stretch of land where previously, and very recently at that, had sat ad hoc impromptu temporary corrugated-roofed hangars and neat mown airstrips, all of which were gone and gone as if they'd never even been present in the first place.

Though I walked through these moments assured within my very stones and bones these were the very moments of my life, only a fool wouldn't have considered the seemingly impossible possibility that one might have, via some slip of the wit of the world, taken a step back in Time a half-decade or so, or to the contrary, might just have stepped forwards in Time fifty years into the future, but such was the rot, surely it would take the elements of the world a hundred years at least to bring such a fine manor house so low, and as low as it had been brought from just one second to the next.

At a loss for what to do with myself given my present

situation, I was thinking about hopping precarious holes in the floorboards to place myself once more upon the second-storey landing I'd previously had an escort at my side when last I'd walked it, but as it played out, I noticed Wing Command Raven Mocker's curious broken artefact and thinking better about just abandoning this thing to the elements, I picked it back up off of the rotten decrepit-now dresser I'd previously set it down upon, hardly realizing that before I'd even touched it, but not before I was returned to within a few feet of this thing, the manor house restored itself as if by Magic to all of its former stately glory.

'There you are!' said a voice from the doorway causing me to turn around to see it was my damned ranker of an escort. 'This isn't the place to be wandering around without an escort lad! What the devil did you think you were playing at?'

'I'm not entirely sure I actually went anywhere at all actually,' I told him.

'The devil you didn't. Turned my eye from you for a ruddy-muddy second and you just up and vanished lad.'

I looked at the broken shaft of wood in my hand, and though I might have considered more than I did, had I actually been afforded some mind-time to myself, as it was, my escort seemed keen to get back to whatever other duties he would otherwise have been attending to had I, upon this day, not just turned up out of the blue so to speak, thus unsettling things behind the seams of all of the goings on here at RAF Skysong more than I could possibly have realized at this time.

Dressed and refreshed now, I was escorted back to the

manor house lobby, where it seemed the soldier entrusted with my re-imagining of sorts, clearly didn't know what was to be done with me, once he'd done with me what he'd been told to do with me. 'You stay right there my lad,' he told me, and with that said, he disappeared from my line-of-sight of him and that was that. I was an hour just stood there, ignored, neglected, overlooked though I was passed a dozen times by a dozen different enlisted men, mostly officers of indistinguishable rank and regiment as it seemed to my untrained and unschooled eye and mind where The Royal Air Force was concerned, they were though, given the stylized cut of their uniforms, all Royal Air Force, that much at least the uniforms of these rarefied characters spoke in silent volumes.

Certainly I did not know a Flight Commander from a Flight Lieutenant any more than I could tell a Flight Lieutenant from a Flying Officer or a Flying Officer from anyone else now that I come to think about it.

I watched through the great manor doors, late afternoon slowly succumbing to early evening and that activity around the stationary Spitfires winding down to aircrews hopping onto the backs of flatbed trailers being towed by ground crew jeeps, but not once did I see a refueling tanker or any obvious bombs or ammunition changes taking place which I would have thought a norm where airfields on obvious war-footings were concerned. Here though, at RAF Skysong that just didn't appear to be the case. But at the time, I was sure that I imagined it was just because I hadn't actually witnessed such things presuming such things as fuel and fresh bullets had all walked the boards behind my back no doubt.

After all, planes I supposed don't fly on empty tanks, and machine guns can't be fired without ammunition, but then again, where such things as that were concerned, my head and my knowledge and expectations of such things were very much still rooted in what I came to appreciate, or at least see with my new eyes, was a much more mundane way of looking at things truly of a more Magical nature than I'd ever given them credit for in the past.

Everything is made out of Magic.

Even Magic is made out of Magic.

Even the clouds, and that, is where you might as well begin your aviation training, for it was with clouds my mind was first trained into seeing a thing as the thing that it is, a Magic no matter how mundane a thing thee previously supposed it, even if one had never even supposed ought about anything where any particular thing was concerned. Abstract is best for beginners, like sunset and sunrise for both can be said to be so obviously mundane, and Magical be this daily event, before which Mankind of old was humbled for millennia without count, whether this ancient Man had eyes for Magic or not, in the eyes of the beholder alone.

Magic that know Magic, and Magic that begets Magic.

As yet everything was sights and sounds and a brand new sense within my stones and bones that I'd taken my first small step into something I would soon find myself striding headlong straight into. The Royal Air Force's need for Magical pilots being such, my insight alone into this best kept secret saw me fast-tracked straight through recruitment and thrown immediately into my first mission: But that, as a thing I was to endure, like a rite of initiation of sorts, proved a very useful trick designed to expedite matters considerably where setting one's inner Magic free was concerned, by design, given there was little enough time to waste.

This was war remember, and I'd gone and fallen into a secret there truly would otherwise have been no just walking away from. I, as it turned out, was very fortunate indeed, given that faith and trust and hope that was placed in me paid off spectacularly, not least of all for Airman Spellchaser who won the sweepstakes where my inner Totem was concerned.

It was just shy of dusk, I know, I could see the sky through the door and tall windows, when finally the officer and a gentleman I'd met previously, Group Captain Willoughby-Chase, presented himself in the lobby and declared sharply- 'Ah! There you are!'

'Arthur Bird sir,' I told him again.

'Well no fear my boy, we'll make a full bird out of you in no time at all. You'll be coming with me lad!'

'As you say sir.'

'No need to call me sir lad. Not yet at least. Needs must and all that my boy. We'll just have to wait and see if you can be of some use to us first.'

'Use sir?'

'Service lad! To King and to Country!'

'Anything sir. Just say the word sir.'

'You eaten lad?'

'Excuse me sir? I mean- No, sorry. I haven't eaten today at all and not since late supper last night sir. About ten o'clock sir.'

'What was?'

'Late supper sir. Lamb stew sir.'

'Well not saying we might muster up such a fare as I'm sure that was- Lamb stew you say?'

'My aunt,' I said. 'Over at The Bird Farm sir. 'Bout forty miles north I guess, seeing as I followed the Seagull south as it seemed to my sense of the sun.'

'Pilot needs a good sense of the sun lad!' he told me, leading me outside and into the early throws of a picturesque dusk and the general setting of the sun over this day and this airfield and sprawling airbase. There was a jeep with a couple of Air Force MPs already aboard, one in the driver's seat and one already in the back. 'Make sure the lad gets some evening fare,' the officer told the MPs. 'I'll meet you at the mess tent, and then we'll get on with it.'

'Get on with it sir?' I questioned.

'All good things lad!' he said to that.

'All good things sir?'

'Come to those who wait!' he proclaimed. 'But that's just the trick of it lad. We've no time to spare for waiting. No time at all for such things my boy. Trust me. Things will be expedited! It never fails to work, unless of course Arthur lad, you intend to be the first to fail so miserably you'll leave us with no choice but to have to-'

'Send me home sir? Please don't send me home sir,' I said, interjecting my words into whatever point he had himself been about to make.

'Well, as to that lad. Now that you've seen our little white secret here- It won't be home you'll be going.'

'Come again sir.'

'Upon my good advice lad. Don't fail the test. And all will be well with the world, which is your world, from a certain point of view. We are after all lad, at war don't you know. Desperate times and all that.'

'Desperate times sir?'

'Insist upon desperate measures.'

'This test is a desperate measure?'

'By Jove I think the lad's finally getting it!' boasted the officer. 'Look at it this way Arthur my lad. See it as no more than being thrown into the pool at the deep end.'

'The deep end sir. Right you are sir.'

'Either learn to swim lad. Or drown.'

'Drown sir?'

'Figure of speech lad. Not saying we're going to drown you. Not saying you don't already know how to swim. You'll see, This time tomorrow Arthur! You'll belong to a brave and grave new world indeed. Expect lad! Unexpected things! Magic and Miracles my boy! Magic and Miracles! Turn out to be both, and well, you'll end up the most celebrated lad on the base most likely.'

That said, I was driven to the mess tent for evening dinner, and ate a hearty fare amongst at least a dozen officers, who were Spitfire pilots, all of whom were looking at me curiously. I was not spoken to though, and for my part I sat alone with the MPs whom the other pilots, all of them Spitfire pilots, didn't have all that much to do with. I met not a single one of them upon this night, nor spoke to anyone at all. I certainly noted though, even upon this initial occasion, that that peddled and promoted propaganda truth of the average age of a Spitfire fighter pilot was just nineteen, for I saw no such game lads as that sat around the officers' tables. All seemed mature grown men to me, such as sported moustaches and beards no nineteen year old had thus far lived long enough to cultivate upon what ought otherwise to be so fresh a face, it was a wonder they'd even started to shave yet.

These officers seemed of a different caliber entirely, to such as a headstrong youthful dare-devil hell-raiser ready willing and able to risk all for King and Country and quite naturally the thrill of the kill, as I.

They seemed a heady graven bunch these gentlemen, and there were horrors and hopes in their eyes the likes of which I did not know the human face was capable of sporting, or emoting, or more importantly, harboring behind the eyes of a man, but all was there in their eyes to be seen. One just had to take the time, given this once in a lifetime opportunity I actually had to look a fighter pilot in the eyes. Every dogfight they'd ever lived to never speak of again, was there in their eyes, because such things I can suppose now that I know such things, remain with thee in thy heart, that stores such things as wings and prayers and dogfights, those these men walked away from and those dogfights their friends and fellow countrymen didn't.

And all of their eyes seemed fixed upon me, in silence.

And maybe even reverence, but I concede now that might just have been my imagination.

I just ate my dinner, drank my tea and was finally done just as the officer I'd been waiting for arrived to see to it I was, for what was left of this night on earth, appropriately situated for the test of all tests, the greatest test I had ever experienced the endurance of thus far in my life to date. And not no one actually warned me, much.

Again, one MP took to the driver's seat, and the second MP restored himself to the backseat once more. I joined this fellow in the back of the jeep, for the officer took to the passenger seat in the front, and then we sped away, all the way to the very far outskirts of the furthest airstrip where RAF Skysong ended and farmlands began. I was taken alongside the edge of the field and marched out like a man about to face a firing post as it seemed to me, especially as there was indeed a crossed-post of sorts, and indeed towards this post of sorts I was marched almost but not quite, entirely without a word said at all.

'Don't be nervous lad,' the officer told me. 'Not exactly conventional but there's little enough time for ought else and no one else spare to do ought otherwise with you.'

'I'm not sure I follow you sir.'

'Well of course you don't lad, but as it is, you might say of this little sideshow enterprise of ours- We're off to see the Wizard. In that lad, we're just going to have to wait and see just what kind of Wizard you really are. Just what kind of a Wizard you might yet turn out to be. We need good Wizards lad. Don't need anything else but that lad. Wizards!' he said, before saying to those MPs who'd followed us into the crop field- 'Right you are boys. Strap him up and make sure someone comes back for him in the morning.'

'The morning sir?' I questioned, given I'd already worked out strap him up meant just that, for I was strapped to the crossbar of the post, like a scarecrow in such a fashion, I would not particularly easily, or successfully for that matter, free myself from this ad hoc impromptu incarceration even if I had the mind to, which I'm sure I did from time to time throughout the night.

'Aye lad. It's a simple thing really. All you have to do is scare away the crows.'

'Crows sir? What crows?'

'Oh there's always crows in this field lad. You just wait and see.'

'Wait and see what? Crows?'

'Wait and see if you have it in you lad to actually scare a single ruddy-muddy crow off. Scare them all away and no doubt someone will see them scattering and come and see how you are. Morning most likely lad. So you've got the entire night to think about it.'

'Think about it? Think about what?'

'Well whether or not it's likely to rain tonight would be a start but given this summer we're stuck with, rain I think will be the last thing upon your mind.'

'And what exactly ought I to be considering instead?' I asked after an obvious enquiring nature, one that surely wouldn't so easily be satiated short of some better explanation being afforded me concerning this coming trial by stars as it seemed to me at this time.

'Crows my boy! Crows and corn!'

'Right you are then sir,' I said. 'Crows and corn.' At this point, so securely fastened to the post, a scarecrow they had made of me, and that it seemed was that, and that said, this and precisely this was all the welcome I received from RAF Skysong. All three of them made an about turn and departed I presumed for they left me facing the expanse of crop fields ahead of me whilst they walked behind my back, back to the jeep and from the sound of it, they drove off without any further to do at all upon their part. And that was that suddenly, for there I was, in a field surrounded by an abundant plenty of uncut crops for as far as my eyes could see, with naught but the entire stretch of this night in its entirety to contemplate this most curious and unexpected eventful end to a very eventful day indeed, if not a whole day and half the night previous.

Certainly far more than I'd gone to bed expecting of the night and the following morrow had since occurred to so throw my life this tangent curve I was yet to be so entirely spun by the centrifugal forces thereof as to be left dizzy and gasping for air. Nor was I entirely drowning yet in this world I had been literally thrown into the deep end thereof, seemingly upon this night under an ocean of stars, to either sink, or swim. When what would mean to sink, or equally perplexing as yet, just what it might actually mean to swim from this, back to the shores of sanity so to speak. As it was, come what may, I was in this till the end regardless, having come this far, to end up a scarecrow, so I would be left to see, if I actually had it in me to actually scare a single crow into the sky, let alone any greater number of crows than that.

Naturally I thought I might just call and caw in such a fashion as to startle with these vocalized hoots and hollers whatever crow might show themselves, but upon lengthy reflection and mental mind-based interrogation of the strange nature of this test, for it was a test and I'd been told as much, as plain and true as that, surely it stood to reason that in being a test, it was surely not going to prove any easy feat?

Somewhere within the design of this nocturnal endurance, surely there must have actually been a test? Perchance a riddle to be solved, the solution to which oneself surely already in possession thereof, otherwise how might this be a test of ought or anything but one's willingness to go along with whatever, just as long as oneself as a soldier has been ordered to do whatever it is one had been ordered to do? Certainly that would, perhaps prove thyself an apt and astute soldier of a sort? The sort of soldier who does as he's told, regardless of what it is he has been told to do, even die, just as long as it comes down the chain of command, the buck stopping dead with said soldier, be it wartime or be it teatime or what-not or whatever time.

But then again, this wasn't the army.

This was The Royal Air Force, and clearly this secret airfield of theirs did things differently, after all, it sported a whole Squadron of Dragon Spitfires, and that, at least in my eyes upon this night on earth, surely would come to count for everything.

5

FOR WHOM THE WIND BLOWS

I don't suppose they knew I could hear them, but I could, and had they known, I doubt a man amongst them would have cared, be they officers and gentlemen or not; albeit Pilot Officer, and Spitfire fighter pilots first and foremost. For this was this night's reveille, this was this night's early evensong, and they were celebrating, as I was to come to learn they did every single night, or at least, for all I knew, it was upon this very night that just this very tradition had its immaculate conception? All of them were alive and no one was dead, the fate of Wing Commander Raven Mocker surely known amongst their number now, and besides, I'd already let the cat out of the bag so to speak, via informing any old ground crewman of this fact.

You might suppose then, at least upon this occasion, the truth of it didn't filter down from the highest echelons of this airfield's Command, but up from its most lowest echelon, and latest new recruit upon whom, though I couldn't possibly know it at the time, was steeped so great an expectation. I could hear them from their deckchairs, drinking wine and eating cheese whilst listening to English free radio. From the sound of the voices I heard but the distant-dampened fleeting dispatches thereof, rising and falling and sometimes following whomever to whatever crescendo that resulted in either a punchline I entirely missed the funny to, or likewise, some witty anecdote that escaped the wit of me entirely, and though not everyone was an Englishman, they were though, one and all, of this I was certain, Spitfire Pilots. And thus Dragons. And thus Wizards.

Given that I know now, that which I couldn't possibly have known for sure back then, I see no reason not to utilize this opportunity to just paint a better picture of this night than I was able to paint for myself in my mind at the time: For one I didn't yet know why I had been rendered onto the likeness of a scarecrow, and for two, though I could hear it in their accents, for all conversed the one with another or one with everyone in English, as I have said, in not all being Englishmen, they turned out to be from many a varied and very splendid County indeed, those Wizards who were also fantastical fairy tale Dragons, totemically speaking, in being not from England, were in fact from such very splendid places on earth, as Holland, Belgium, Poland, Norway, Czechoslovakia, France, Scotland, Wales, Ireland, Rhodesia both north and south, Newfoundland, and there were even Spitfire fighter pilots onside from places as exotic as Barbados, Jamaica, Australia, and though not necessarily exotic, from the sound of this man, there was at least one American amongst their number, such as were, and comprised, in full, RAF Squadron No.1: Dragon Squadron.

And though I was to come to learn they were all Pilot

Officer's and very splendid gentleman after many a colorful many-varied splendid bouquet of character and assorted dashing daring dandy panache, they were first and foremost, Wizards!

Warrior Wizards!

Of the most eclectic kind.

I was also sure, as this day dimmed, if I really trained my ears to an even more distant camaraderie, I could hear the subdued evensong of the ground crews, one of whom, if I wasn't mistaken and it wasn't instead the wind, was playing a harmonica. And there was I, strapped to a cross-post so as to play the role afforded me of scarecrow, with naught but a wall of unharvested crop filling the full field of vision of my 270° or so of sight, given I could obviously still turn my neck from side to side. Fortunately, I could also tilt my head back so as to look up, and found myself doing so as I heard first their engines, and then witnessed the spectacle of Seagull Squadron coming in to land, directly over my head.

Twenty-seven Seagulls surely, of which I only saw the underbellies thereof all but in passing, until that was, the post I was strapped to suddenly spun around a full 180° so as to leave me actually looking upon the sheer finesse and majesty with which these Seagulls came in to land, for just like the Dragons, these birds also needed absolutely no runway whatsoever, given they could just land, just like a bird.

The runways it would turn out, were all for taking off.

I saw a man, an officer and a gentleman flourishing in my direction, the same strange slender short-staff of a pilot that I had taken as a souvenir from the Wing Commander, my wounded man himself. That was when I remembered the scarecrow upon my uncle's farm turning at so choice an opportune moment as to catch those bullets meant for me, to the side of which, as I realized now, had been staggering Raven Mocker, flourishing in his own hand, whatever that thing was that he was flourishing so, specifically.

Just like this scarecrow, the scarecrow that was me, just did. Only now as it was, did it strike me odd, that a scarecrow had saved me, and now I was the scarecrow, strapped like a damned stripped-ranker awaiting a firing squad as it felt to me prior to all of my hopes being realized in this instance, amongst other things.

So he'd saved me then: Wing Commander Raven Mocker, he'd saved my life, and taken a bullet for his troubles in doing so.

'Thought you might like to watch- Arthur yes. Arthur Bird.'

'I am Arthur sir.'

'Call me Jonathan,' he told me. A man of about twenty-one years of age.

'That thing in your hand?' I said, meaning to say more and upon the very spur and cusp of having said what I'd already said, and without pause of delay in my delivery of this most obviously lingering question, but as it was, I found I had no need.

'This?' he questioned, performing am aerobatic flip with this baton of a thing before catching it again. 'This Arthur Bird, is my Royal Magical Air Force military-grade military-issue

Magical Decree. Wouldn't want to get shot down over enemy country carrying that Magical Decree set aside for me at birth now would I. It bears ones ruddy-muddy name after all now doesn't it.'

'Does it sir? I mean, Jonathan sir. Does it?'

'You don't have a Magical Decree lad? It would look like this one, only it wouldn't be green, but most likely a splendid varnished wood, and instead of saying what this one says, yours quite naturally would say- Arthur Bird, yes.'

'I own no such thing sir.'

'Well as to that,' he said, flipping once more that thing he was holding in his hand when he wasn't tossing it up and catching it again. 'This is yours lad. Standard practice and all young chap. Not saying it's loaded or anything because it isn't.'

'No sir. I mean yes sir.'

'You really don't know what it is do you?'

'Never saw such a thing in my life I didn't, until just last night. Wing Commander dropped his.'

'Is that how you came to be able to see him?'

'No sir. I saw him long before he dropped this Decree you say, in my uncle's field.'

'And well for us that he did,' said this man. 'Seeing as he's taken himself out of the game for at least a short while, one man down becomes one man up.'

'You mean me?'

'Lad's sharp. And a Wizard who doesn't know-'

'He's a Wizard.'

'Yes well, quite, and as to that old boy- Crash course in Magic coming right up.'

'Really sir.'

'Well, that just depends upon you lad now doesn't it,' he said, stepping aside suddenly so might I better set my eyes, not upon him, but upon those Seagulls coming in to land, Seagulls that were Wizards at the very root, stem, and core of these great giant majestic birds of seaside spectacle.

Seagulls that once stripped of their Wizard, or Wizards as it turned out, seemed a selection of Vickers Wellingtons, Fairey Battle planes, and Westland Lysanders.

And yet, in my mind, the humble Spitfire had been both Dragon, and Sparrow? Because the pilot of the one had been a Dragon, and the pilot of the other, had been a Sparrow. The Spitfire, though two separate planes entirely in this instance, had been but a Spitfire.

'The Sparrow sir.'

'Was me,' he told me.

'You sir?'

'Pilot Officer Jonathan Livingstone at your pleasure young master Arthur Bird. All being well, soon to be Officer Cadet Bird- But, just what kind of a bird is our Bird to turn out to be then? Quite exciting really when you come to think of it. Rumor has it the ground crew chaps are having a little sweepstake on the side. Ten bob down I think to participate. Terribly off regulations and all that old boy, but when needs must, needs must as they say. Keeps everyone's morale up. Which brings us back to you Arthur Bird.' He slipped my very own military-grade military-issue Magical Decree, upon which was writ those very same words I'd previously gleamed for both receiving and believing therein those very words, from Wing Commander Raven Mocker's own Magical Decree, albeit, military-grade military-issue, wand, into my belt, which was also military-grade military-issue.

'I was told I was to scare off the crows Jonathan sir. But-'

'Ah! You're wondering where are the crows aren't you old boy. Well as to crows, who knows where a crow goes when he's off being a crow don't you know.'

'Sir?'

'There'll be crows lad! You mark my words! There will be crows!'

'As you say sir.'

'Might be this time tomorrow old boy, I'll be calling you sir.'

'I'm not sure I follow you sir. How could I possibly-'

'Be the bird you were born to be young master Bird. And scare as many ruddy-muddy crows with it as you can summon yourself to muster from within lad. It'll come from within for what is the without to a Wizard, eh?'

'As you say sir.'

'Any questions old boy?'

'Many and more sir! Many and more!'

'And if I was to permit thee just the one, perchance what might that one question be?'

'A question of Seagulls and Sparrows sir, I'm afraid it would have to be.'

'Clever boy! And a loaded question indeed,' he said, his disposition that of a cheery sort. 'Well, I'll say this young master Bird, as you are now, so were many of us also. Including my good-self old boy don't you know. I too once had to ponder for an entire evensong and morn, with what, precisely, was I going to scare away the crows. As I'm sure it has already occurred to you by now, so too did it once upon a night very much like this one, occur to me. Naturally I thought I might just call and caw in such a fashion as to startle with these vocalized hoots and hollers whatever crow might show themselves, but upon lengthy reflection and mental mind-based interrogation of the strange nature of this test, for it was a test and I'd been told as much, as plain and true as that, surely it stood to reason that in being a test, it was surely not going to prove any easy feat? Somewhere within the design of this nocturnal endurance, surely there must have actually been a test? Perchance a riddle to be solved, the solution to which oneself surely already in possession thereof, otherwise how might this be a test of ought or anything but one's willingness to go along with whatever, just as long as oneself as a soldier has been ordered to do whatever it is one had been ordered to do? Certainly that would, perhaps prove thyself an apt and astute soldier of a sort? The sort of soldier who does as he's told, regardless of what it is he has been told to do, even die, just as long as it comes down the chain of command, the buck stopping dead with said soldier, be it wartime or be it teatime or what-not or whatever time. But then again, this is The Royal Magical Air Force, and clearly at this secret airfield of ours, we do things differently, yes?'

'I should say.'

'Quite, old boy.'

'And you took the thoughts right out of my head sir I swear you did. Nailed it precisely sir.'

'Well of course I did old boy. I was the one who planted the thought into your mind in the first place. Which is both a good thing, and another thing entirely old boy. But now's not the time for that. All that and everything else will come Arthur my boy. Trust me on that. All good things and all.'

'Come to those that wait.'

'And you Arthur Bird my boy, I'm afraid to say, will be waiting for dawn. That is most likely when the crows will show up. Trust in that lad. Or you'll be here for a very long time old boy. A very long time indeed. But look at it this way, having already had you're final meal, you'll die of thirst long before you'll ever get the chance to starve to death.'

'True story sir? You'd all let me die sir?'

'It has not yet ever come to that Arthur my boy. And besides, I think I'll be putting in with the sweepstakes, you know, show some solidarity with the good old boys of the ground crew.'

'Sweepstakes?'

'Random draw is a sweepstakes lad. You pays your ante, you place your bet, and draw from all known and sometimes unknown possibilities, most likely an empty oil can, one's sweepstake.'

'All known and sometimes unknown sir?'

'Possibilities old boy. Birds my boy. Birds. They'll all be birds or ball park don't you know. And besides, if you were a lion or even, let's say, a tiger, you would not have found your way onto this airfield I assure you, with or without the Wing Commander's shattered Decree. You'd have naturally been compelled to find yourself elsewhere if that were so. And after all old boy, you're ruddy-muddy name's Bird after all don't you know.'

'What does that mean?'

'It means old boy, you're not likely now to be a lion or a ruddy-muddy tiger now are you. Not with a name like Bird.'

'My mother's maiden name was Bachelor.'

'Aye and it seems to me she found herself a ruddy-muddy good one eh lad? Seeing as they've given England, you Arthur Bird.'

'England sir?'

'Well, you're here after all now aren't you old boy.'

'And glad to be here.'

'Good. Good, glad can sometimes be enough.'

'Enough?'

'Be the bird you were born to be Arthur. And I guess, I must now suppose there endeth the lesson. I have said to thee as it was put to me. I was the last one in- Until there was you of course.'

'Yes. Now there is me.'

'Trust me my boy. No one will come until we see scattering crows. Do, or die lad.'

'Die?'

'Only way to be sure our little white secret here dies with you.'

'Bit harsh sir, don't you think? I can mop too I'm sure.'

He laughed at that remark, and tapping that Magical Decree he'd slipped me, with his own, he nodded, tipped his cap and bid me adieu.

I did not say to that though, and would not say to that though- Auf Wiedersehen.

With him gone, I found myself looking a moment upon a vast array of some twenty-seven assorted planes, from Fairey Battle planes, to Vickers Wellingstons and Westland Lysanders, all teeming as is with ground crew going through the motions of checks, and I must say I noted once more, the sheer absence of fuel trucks and tankers and any trucks or trolleys or what-not or whatever might have sported reloads for the machine guns, or bombs for the bellies of these planes that soon would be birds once more, but were just planes now, all of which seemed in need of a little spit and elbow polish and all the tender love and care the ground crews, via whatever sentimental attachments of affinity such as they, had for such as these planes, afforded them. As dusk darkened, and night hearkened not, suddenly to the day for the one from the other, could not till dawn, ever be so far removed, which struck me as curious.

I might have looked deeper and for twice as long and seen no doubt twice as far, but just as he was about to pass out of an obvious line of sight with me, insomuch as my line of sight with this Pilot Officer's departing back, I saw him over his shoulder, flourishing his Magical Decree, just a single rotation, and with that, I was turned back around, via Magical means, and naught but a pure Magic as it seemed to me, so as to be once more facing the crops, with not a single crow in sight. But then again, this was but post-dusk and the early throws of the darkness that would become of this night on earth, before dawn, before I could expect such as crows to make my acquaintance.

I was left wondering, given I entirely forgot to question him upon a hundred and one things and more before he was departed, just how it was that some Wizards were Dragons, and he, well, was not I suppose that line of enquiry would have tread the very boards thereof, the theatre of this Sparrow. Nor did I ask him how it was a small number of Wizards would collectively form a Seagull of all things, and not some bigger, bolder, more brazen Dragon perhaps?

But the answer to that question of a conundrum came to me soon enough, when the answer to that question was in itself a question, as in, it was all just a question of Wizards, and numbers, as in, that number of Wizards capable of emoting such as a Dragon, to Spitfires, with little to no surplus I supposed; given that surely, Wizards who were also Dragons would make by far, the very best Spitfire fighter pilots The Royal Magical Air Force could possibly hope to boast amongst their Sky Pilot ranks.

It also occurred to me, The Royal Magical Air Force must surely, my logic being astute as I already knew it was, be one Dragon amiss; said logic stemming from the root that was that flower that was the Spitfire that was both Spitfire, and Sparrow, and not as was surely the golden mean, a Dragon.

Would I then, if I turned out to be a Dragon, automatically take the Spitfire from the Sparrow, rendering him such as might, just as likely end up lending his wings, albeit feathers thereafter, and forever thereafter, or until such a time Spitfires for Sparrows are available, a Seagull?

I interrogated this very curious thought that had just now popped into my mind: If I turned out to be a Dragon.

Curious I thought as it also, upon the back of this, it occurred to me to wonder just how might one, turn out to be a Dragon precisely?

I counted stars for a few hours, by which time, it seemed I had the night to myself for all of the Pilot Officers had fallen so silent, one had to surely presume they'd all retired for the night, presumably to the manor house, along with all of the Wizards of Seagull Squadron, and also, all of the ground crews had also gone silent, wherever it was they bunked or bivouacked on nights such as this one. I counted ten thousand stars and more, and hearkened to the silence of the serenity of this night, myself afloat upon that ocean of stars above, like it be naught but a reflection in the face of a lake, mirroring the stars above, with which I must surely have been myself swimming, given I was looking down upon this twilight world of twinkles looking right back up at me.

It was the night I was the scarecrow.

By daylight true, I would come to be so much more.

Given it was immediately apparent upon the Sparrow's departure, that if I wanted to be a Spitfire fighter pilot, if I wanted to strap on my very own Spitfire, I would have to emote, for surely it would be a thing emoted from within, whatever thing that was already within oneself to be emoted in the first place.

Emoted, I thought.

Unleashed I thought the better expectation.

I played the Wing Commander's final confrontation with his STRICT DISCIPLINARIAN NEMESIS past my mind's eye again and again and again. More so to see these two combatants not as men with their flying boots upon the ground, nor as Wizards or even as Warriors, but as the Dragons they had been.

For they had been Dragons these men.

The fortunate few.

I would be a Dragon too I thought, but how I might manifest before such as crows, a Dragon, as yet I had no idea, but as it was as yet, I still had the stretch of the reach of this night to think about it.

Certainly I thought about it, and thought about it as hard as I could, and for as long as I could, succinctly, without my mind wandering onto other less pressing things, so much so, I thought myself so focused upon this fantasy of a fairy tale fiction of a real world thing, until myself distracted.

And by distracted I mean reset to counting stars.

I thought I saw my brother, Claude, but surely I couldn't have seen my brother, for Claude was dead, dead but not buried yet I imagined, but dead for sure. I'd seen his charred crisp cadaver of a burnt and blackened and soot-streaked corpse still glistening with dying embers around the edges of those patches of pyjama as good as smoldered to his flesh by the flames, to such a degree one could not tell pyjama from flesh or exposed flesh from pyjama. All was black. All was death.

His ghost then surely?

For it was not a flesh blood and bones and stones apparition of my brother, but my brother as a ghostly form, seemingly made out of moonlight, or at least, seen via some unknown previously unremarked upon correlation between ghost sightings and the presence of moonlight, or at least some medium of a veil upon which such as a ghost might project itself, or be seen, like a thing walking across a screen? Be that moonbeams and moon glow or sunbeams and sun glow, or perchance in old dusty houses, the dust itself the medium by which such as a ghost might be seen, or incense even or just simple smoke?

I did not know for I could not know.

Not having been raised to be a Wizard.

Was that what it was that I'd just now seen, wandering for weaving in and out of the tall stalks upon the very peripheral edge of that farmland I was myself gazing into, deeply, and long, and long enough for my mind to start playing tricks upon my eyes?

I decided to blink, and he was gone.

I did not call out to him. I had no care to concern myself with such as thoughts unleashed upon the prowess of which, even be these things voiced at little more than a whisper or less, would so shatter the silence of the world, such as silence might never again settle over the world in my lifetime. The silence was good, and no less suddenly serene for the owl that hooted once, only to hoot again. Least it was two owls conversing the one with the other, out there in the distant darkness, upon which surely, this darkness both brightened and lightened by that blanket silver lining, laid upon all that the moon with this light, and with this love, caressed.

Myself included.

Moon and stars and me.

Hours passed. Dark became dawn and dawn became day and I heard RAF Skysong wake up, get up, and get on with the day and counted the early hours thereof stretched to high noon, given I could see the sun and the sun could see me; within which time, Dragon Squadron took to the sky but did not fly east for I thought myself surely facing east. And well you may ask, if I did not see this Squadron departing, how is it that I know it was Dragon Squadron departing and not another? But the answer to that ought already to be obvious, for I heard both Squadrons departing, this airfield's every single plane, though not a single pilot flew their Magic over my head on this day.

I did presume though, seeing as I was yet to see a single crow, and afternoon reached eventually early evening, I would soon, if not see all of these planes returning, I would surely soon hear them all returning. A plane after all needs refueling and re-arming- But no, I'd seen no refueling trucks, nor had I seen a single plane armed with ought but a wing and a prayer, at least, to my knowledge. I did though, have my back to their morning salutations, and then they were gone, and as of now, the early evening thereof this day I'd spent baking in the hot sun, not a single plane was back.

Dusk became dawn and dawn became day and day disappeared under a fog so thick, I could not see the wheat for this chaffing molasses of deep thick even cloud, sunk so low as to bring low the whole world as it seemed to me. A wet fog that left me dripping in rain though not a single drop of rain had fallen. I was though, left refreshed, and anything put the parched baked dead-soon scarecrow I was fast becoming. And still no plane returned, but then again, what with the fog I didn't suppose any plane would, need they runway or not, for surely they'd all been diverted to some other airfield, should such as the secret Magical Air Force, such as did not share ought more in common with the Royal Air Force than that, that they were both Air Forces, a second secret Magical airfield somewhere?

Behind this molasses of mist, day became night, and night faded finally to dawn, to which I awoke, having been asleep on my feet, and dreaming. In my dream I thought I could hear a single plane making a pass overhead, and of this dawn, I heard it too. A single plane, out there somewhere in the thinning slowly lifting cloud. Whoever it was, they were coming in low, presumably to land I supposed until I got a terrible sense of dread suddenly. Having been looking up, I suddenly found myself looking down, not down at the ground but at the harvest and not really at the harvest but at those few hundred crows that suddenly seemed to appear from nowhere, settled suddenly wherever there seemed a thing sturdy enough for a crow to settle upon it. Behind their silence, the single plane sounded close, and close enough ahead of me to suppose a pilot coming in low over the very heads of the harvest stalks, through the fog of which I thought I might suddenly see a Sparrow perhaps?

It was not a Sparrow though. It was a *CROW*.

A giant black *STRICT DISCIPLINARIAN CROW*!

I raged! I couldn't help myself and found myself waking up seemingly the very next second in a hospital bed, within a makeshift Field Hospital, the day never bluer behind a kindly nurse who seemed to have been expecting me. 'Ah, there you are master Bird. It's about time you woke up,' she said, plumping up my pillows for me as I lay there, once more dressed in pyjamas, but this time, these pyjamas weren't my own: From the look of them, standard hospital issue. 'You've been keeping your visitor waiting all morning you have master Bird.'

'Visitor?' I asked, this an obvious thing to say I thought, as was- 'Claude.' For having sat up, there he was, my visitor, stood at the foot of my hospital bed. It was Claude. My brother. And he was alive.

6

THE TOP SECRET JOY OF FLIGHT

'You realize I'm dead don't you?' he said to me, my twin brother, Claude that is, and that said, I suddenly found myself awoken by the sound of a Mosquito if I thought I knew the sound of my RAF planes in service at this time well enough to know one plane from another, to discover myself abed in what was obviously, the very same Field Hospital of my dream.

There was no expectant nurse though, and no one to stop me getting out of bed to wander outside, which was outside of the tent I'd awoken in, technically, regained consciousness in, as in, came round within to find day had dawned bright and blue, and that single plane that was come, was already landed upon a field adjacent to the field I currently found myself within. First things first though, I'd checked my bedside for personal belongings and found only the military-grade military-issue wand I'd been handed, but thus far, as far as I was aware, had yet to actually earn.

I could see a town I didn't recognize a half mile away, and

an army base as good as sprawling all around me, but as it was, no one paid me any attention whatsoever as I walked towards that already harvested field upon which that pilot currently heading more or less in my direction, had landed a Mosquito. It's familiar red, white and blue roundel sang a silent patriotic dispatch to my every sense of a sense and more, and I knew, I just knew, this pilot was here for me. 'Officer Cadet Bird I presume,' he said to me once I'd headed him off at the hedge between his field and my field, until his field became our field and there I was, stood right in front of him.

'Is it that obvious sir?'

'What, that you can see me?'

'You mean they can't?' I said, meaning that field full of army personnel coming and going about their business in the field and all of the expanse of the field behind me now.

'We wouldn't be much of a Secret Air Force now would we Officer Cadet Bird, if we could be seen by just anyone.'

'Then how is it that I can see you?'

'For one. You're a Wizard. And two. You hold there in your hand a Royal Air Force-'

'Wand,' I said, suddenly supposing to place, or at least, imbue, my idea of just such as that, with such as this thing he had mentioned.

'Yes well, you won't be needing it today-'

'Arthur,' I said.

'Actually,' he said. 'Old sport. You're in The Royal Magical Air Force now. And as a matter of fact, it's Pilot Cadet Bird.

Best get used to it.'

'Already am,' I told him, for I already was. Who wouldn't be? 'And you are sir?'

'Group Captain Peregrine Falcon!' he said, sternly but not so strict as he might otherwise have been.

'Really sir. The Group Captain himself has come for me?'

'As to that Pilot Cadet. I have. Myself being just one of some few Group Captains with naught better to do than find one of our wayward strays, and see him back to The Home Nest.'

'Home nest sir? What's home nest?'

'Skysong Cadet! Why Skysong Manor of course!'

'Then- It wasn't a dream?' I asked, not really meaning to but I said it regardless whether it was meant as a question or not.

'What wasn't a dream?'

'RAF Skysong sir, I mean, Group Captain sir. And my finding my way there with word of Wing Commander Raven Mocker's fate sir.'

'Contrary to your miraculous adventure some few days ago lad, and all those spades it paid off in-'

'Spades sir?'

'Aces lad! Aces!' he enthused, seemingly quite jovial a moment before it passed. 'You found us Cadet. We didn't find you. You, you might say, are a bit of a first for old Blighty don't you know.'

'A first sir?'

'First Wizard already imbued with such flights of fancy

109

would make even half a Wizard as he, a very valuable asset indeed.'

'Valuable asset?'

'Well seeing as you haven't yet been introduced to the subtle nuances and etiquette and customs becoming of a Magical Air Force Cadet, we'll just get on with it shall we?'

'Get on with it sir?'

'Follow me,' he said, and that said, he made an about turn and we walked hereafter side by side the mile of field from the inner-face of the sunbaked withered hedgerow, to this man's Mosquito. This man who was both a man and a Group Captain, one whose name was Peregrine Falcon, such as no doubt made him perfect for The Magical Royal Air Force, seeing as he was both a Wizard and a descendant of ornithological breeding presumably with a name like that. For my name was Bird, and I'd already been told, upon account of that, ornithological my inner Spirit Being would be. Such as some call, Totem, and others call, other things.

Thing is, when you want to communicate a thing to someone, all you have to do is follow the simple singular golden rule, and only rule, when it comes to communicating anything with anyone, and it really doesn't matter just who it is, just as you follow, as I have said, the simple golden rule: Speak the same language as the person you're trying to communicate with.

Be that language what-not or whatever, verbal, sign, semaphore, signifier, signal fire, smoke and mirrors, bells and whistles or just plain, common English. As it was, we were speaking one Royal Magical Air Force man to another.

As we walked, I found myself free to wonder, and so free to make free with my questions, for he said nothing about any count of questions that once used up, would forbid me from ever asking him another. 'Might I not enquire Group Captain,' I said, supposing myself addressing this man, given his rank, compared to mine own, well enough to be getting on with it as he'd suggested.

'Well out with it Cadet or just hold that thought until you think to put it to another. You won't be with me long.'

'I was just wondering Group Captain, how is it I came to find myself waking up in yonder field in an obviously army Field Hospital?'

'Don't know. Don't care,' he said. 'I was just told to follow my compass and see where you'd got to, and all being well, fly you back to Skysong with me.'

'All being well?'

'You're alive aren't you?'

'Yes sir.'

'Then all's well Cadet,' he said.

'And by follow your compass?' I asked.

He handed me a compass, common military-issue, only the needle of this thing seemed affixed upon me, and my chest, I know because I turned around as we walked a few times and always the compass remained fixed upon me, in a truly mostly mysterious and presumably Magical way. 'How?' I found myself both thinking and asking.

'Only need your name Cadet Bird. Arthur Bird. And a most celebrated bird you are indeed.'

'Bird sir? Celebrated sir?'

'Well, as to that, yes and no.'

'Yes and no?' I questioned, as seemed an obvious thing to do, given he seemed somewhat unnecessarily cryptic as it seemed to me.

'Celebrated by everyone upon the entire base Cadet, and especially so, I believe by Pilot Officer Spellchaser whom cleaned up upon the sweepstakes; quite the tidy sum I'm told. Don't advocated or endorsee it, but can't condone it lad. No sense sticking one's nose where it doesn't belong yes.'

'And the no sir?'

'Well, as to that, there is one fellow back at Skysong who's not exactly celebrating your exemplary display of ferocious heroics just the other day.'

'Who?'

'Why the very ruddy-muddy German fellow piloting the German Crow you grounded just the other day of course.'

'Other day? How long have I been missing sir?'

'Aye, missing and not AWOL which is lucky for you. And besides, wouldn't make any sense to court martial our newest recruit before he's even been told he's in now would it.'

'In sir?'

'In The Royal Air Force Cadet. Pay attention now. You've been recruited, enlisted, and afforded the rank, Cadet Pilot.'

'Who me sir. Thank you sir. Won't let you down sir.'

'King and Country Cadet! King and Country first young lad.'

'I'm seventeen sir. Just sir.'

'I'm very aware of that Cadet. We all are. Thing is Cadet Bird, had Pilot Officer Livingstone realized he'd just encountered, upon encountering you, Cadet Bird, the most powerful Wizard to rise out of England for generations, most likely in the world for an Age, he might have chosen his words more wisely.'

'His words sir?'

'His welcome then. Perhaps then, it wouldn't now fall to me to break it to you Cadet Bird.'

'Break what to me Group Captain?'

'Your terrible tragic and truly terrifying new reality Cadet of course. You my boy, just became our most treasured jewel in the crown. You my boy, are a rare kind of Bird indeed.'

'I don't remember sir.'

'Well of course you don't Cadet. You've been under a Spell don't you know. And you still are and will be until such a time as this Spell that you're under has been broken. And it is not for me to lift it. I'm just your chauffer.'

'Chauffer?'

'Pilot then,' he told me as we reached his Mosquito.

'I'm excited sir,' I told him, not sure of the etiquette of such things but upon saying that, I just thought he might actually like to know.

'Good Cadet. Good. Sometimes excited can be enough.'

'Enough sir? Enough for what?'

'To place oneself in that harm's way one most certainly has coming Cadet. Trust me upon that.'

'Harm's way sir?'

'Cadet! We're at ruddy-muddy war lad! And you're in The Magical Air Force now my son. And given what I've been told, and you haven't yet, you're going to be put through Flight School ASAP Cadet Bird. Rest assured lad, the sooner you earn your wings the better off we'll all be.'

'Better off?'

'Country and King lad. Country and King. Not to mention all of us.'

'All of us?'

'All those fellow Pilot Officers' lives you're going to save before we're done with the ruddy-muddy German.'

'I'm going to save lives?'

'Wizard like you Cadet- Is sure to.'

'Then I'm to make Pilot Officer myself?'

'You will if every single man and woman back at Skysong has anything to do with it Cadet Bird. We need you my son! Believe you me we need you.'

'Thank you for saying so Group Captain.'

'Don't ruddy-muddy thank me lad! When I say harm's way. I mean into combat Cadet. Into a Spitfire and into the sky and into this war and combat, one-on-one with such German Wizards who will not go quietly into the night, but will rage at you like you've never known such as rage in your entire life before.'

'Rage?'

'Seventeen you say?'

'Just,' I said to that.

'Miraculous,' he remarked, looking me up and down as I stood there upon the field in my pyjamas. 'Quite simply Miraculous!' That said, we climbed aboard and I took to the secondary seat as he strapped himself into the pilot's. My back to him, I did not see him insert his Magical Decree into the receptacle for this thing, such as turned this Enchanted Magical object into this pilot's, and thus this Mosquito's, flight stick. I was donning my flight helmet at the time, one that accommodated within its apt design, a radio so might I communicate with the pilot and thus, so the pilot would be able to communicate with me.

As I didn't yet speak this man's language, the language of The Royal Magical Air Force, I said nothing, and awaited the moment when next I'd been actually spoken to first.

The moment was Magical. The moment was an experience. And the experience was Magical. My first time in a Mosquito, and though I surely thought myself destined and fated via all of my life's entire good fortunes, to pilot one day my very own Spitfire, this wasn't to be the last time I was aboard a Mosquito, but it was the very last time I ever flew a Mosquito as a pillion passenger. The very next time I'd climb aboard a Mosquito, I'd do so as the pilot, with a very special co-pilot indeed flying shotgun with me. For we, meaning myself and the ghost of my brother Claude, were, though I couldn't know it yet, but he, may very well already have made the realization, were destined to together, become both Legends of The Royal Magical Air Force, and the very Battle of Britain itself.

Not The Battle of Britain of historical infamy, fought between the more mundane Royal Air Force and the **German Luftwaffe**, that was fought in our skies more or less simultaneously, but that Battle of Britain that was fought, in the sky, Wizard against Wizard.

English Wizard, and Wizards of varying Nationality but alongside England all the way regardless, against those dark dire strict disciplinarian **BLACK MAGIC WIZARDS** and **SORCERERS** and **MAGICIANS** and such folks of an **ENCHANTED ILK** our ruthless totalitarian **FASCIST** enemy, **EVIL** incarnate on earth itself, as it is in **HELL**, our **ENEMY**, that beast of many heads and hidden hands that would turn out to be **THE ENEMY** of the entire human race, be they Wizard or be they not yet a Wizard awake but a Wizard asleep, pitted against us.

Sublime I should say, and that said, I'll say no more for there is not a word in the worlds, or concept more befitting or becoming all that the very word sublime should, within the very heart of this word, conjure within thine own heart, be thee to thy heart and this word true, the sublime.

Such was Magical Enchanted flight.

The Mosquito transformed for transfiguring itself into a Falcon, and beating its wings, we were airborne before the very wonder of watching this flying machine become such as a

Peregrine Falcon had even faded.

We climbed to this Magical Enchanted otherworldly-seeming Mosquito's optimal ceiling, that remained from within, just a Mosquito whereas upon its outside, it was a Falcon, and soaring like a bird of prey across the face of this day's blue. It was whilst we were soaring, that I noticed that receptacle for such as a Royal Magical Air Force military-grade military-issue wand within my own cockpit, and immediately found myself wondering.

Group Captain Peregrine Falcon's voice spoke to me through my helmet, straight into my ears. 'I know what you're thinking Cadet. But don't do it. No need upon this flight to earn you're wings lad. No need on this flight at all. You just sit back, relax, and enjoy the view.'

'No need sir?'

'Haven't got the ruddy-muddy Betsy of an idea what it'll do Cadet and don't want to know. Not sure I could take it to be honest with you. You being that which you are, and well, one's good self, being, well, just a bird of prey by comparison. Not saying I couldn't accommodate your Magic Cadet. I just don't want to.'

'Say again Group Captain?'

'Questions you may feel free to ask. And be myself free to answer such questions as you might yet dream up, I will do so. You have my word as an officer and a gentleman of The King's own Royal Magical Air Force.'

'No. No questions Group Captain.'

'No questions Cadet?' he questioned.

'Thought I might sit back and relax first Group Captain,' I said, given we'd not been airborne and sky-bound for much more than a few minutes or so.

'Relax to this then,' he said, and from the tone of him I thought he might have been about to put out over my helmet's earphones, English free radio, but instead he introduced me to the top secret joy of flight, as in, the full maneuverable capabilities and sky-prowess of one Mosquito fighter plane sporting in likeness and outer look, that of a giant Peregrine Falcon, this thing a bird of prey indeed.

I experienced every trick in the Flight School book of tricks and then some and more, and even more yet I supposed, given this pilot's seemingly unorthodox attitude and aptitude for aerial artistry, the very science of which was one of this talented pilot's skill-sets.

We looped the loop. We barrel rolled. We twisted and corkscrewed and soared and dived-dived-dived and always came out of whatever aerial display of flight artistry and excellence in style with a well-practiced skill and grace and finesse and pilot panache I was spellbound to experience so up close and personal as this pillion passenger ride, backseat as it was and almost armchair by like comparison if I am to compare it to ought but ten thousand and one and more dreams once had, never truly shelved by thy mind so as to find these things, these dreams, by thy mind forgotten.

And as was I a Wizard, so too was he.

All my dreams come true and more.

Like a dream my life suddenly became, and it was here, now, and right here, right now, in my heart, and my head, that I truly felt I came to earn my wings, despite as it was, right there, right then so to speak, not yet having been informed, or introduced to, such as that bird I was; the very bird I was born to be. The bird that had already made me the most celebrated soul at Skysong, which, if I remembered well enough, is where I'd been before regaining consciousness to find myself, in a bed, in a Field Hospital, living up to its name in that it was actually found to be in a field, some hundred miles away as it seemed to me, seeing as from our height, it was like I could see for miles and miles in every direction.

Pure éclaircisement. Pure indulgence. Pure Fantasy.

But as real as any fact, you would call a fiction.

This was Magic! And we were Wizards.

We were flying. I was flying. The Mosquito was flying. And it was wonderful. So blue the sky and so white the distant clouds and so distant the ground that seemed a patchwork blanket of many varied and shaded summer colors and greens and roads and villages and tiny steeples and spires of Old England's countryside churches. It was beautiful. When we soared, I soared too, and that- That was the best thing of all. The soaring. The soaring and gliding upon wide stretched unfurled wings, surfing the sky and those invisible currents of air a talented pilot just senses, like thee imbued with a seventh sense for such things, all par for the majesty of the gift of flight.

7

SPELL'S BELLES
DANCING IN THE DARK

I will now, for the sake of expediting my tale, condense with this chapter of my life, thy days alive on earth to such a degree, much ground will be covered with as few choice words as I can think to shrink via whatever literary craft I possess, restricting thy desire to count both the very seconds and minutes and hours of my life over the next few months to naught but passing remark.

For what was May, must soon become September though 'twas July 10th the battle really began in earnest and 31st October when the battle finally lost all of its momentum as it seemed to us, despite the enemy's campaign continuing on to the end of May 1941 from their point of view, when the enemy finally decided to stop wasting planes over England, our defenses being such, by then, the enemy planes didn't last long against us, nor were they able to commit to these sky conflagrations, the same number of planes nor the same level of commitment to the fight as the enemy had mustered across previous months of glorious expectations upon their part, brought low by that part we played in bringing said expectations so low in the first place.

They were though, at first determined, until finally distracted and then ultimately withdrawn from the conflict with England to better serve their extended cause in that campaign our enemy launched not against England thereafter, but Russia instead, and that, as they say, was that. Mankind's common MAD-MAD-MAD-MAD-MAD enemy was never able to recover from that dire gamble.

God bless Winter.

God bless Russia.

It all started though, the ultimate inevitable downfall, be it the downfall and not just the releasing of Germany from this HIDDEN HAND'S grip there upon, such as Germany, of this GREAT EVIL of our times, in the sky over England, with a few brave men, outnumbered damn near 10:1, that it was truly decided.

True Story!

May 1941 was the month the enemy finally gave up, though it was July 10th 1940, that being the day, the month, the year, our enemy first set in motion, a battle for the skies over England that was to make Legends & Heroes of those few brave men of both The Magical, and the less-magical but truly no less magical mundane Royal Air Force that also stood the line, and faced this ever looming threat to the life and liberty of all of their fellow ground-based countrymen, be they soldiers or civilians or what-not or whatever; Magicians, Sorcerers, Wizards and folks of an otherwise Enchanted Otherworldly ilk, mostly, and all of those souls far less Magical than they ought to have been from their own points of view, and those souls, so Magical, such titles as Magician, Sorcerer or even Wizard so fails to capture the Spirit of such souls, I have not the appreciation of The Celestial Realms nor their mechanics to do such souls as these any literary justice at all, period. But they were there too, standing the line, fighting the fight, behind the seams of all of our dreams, laboring to do naught but keep the dream alive in as many hearts as possible, truly, given *THE EVIL* that had raised, like a hydra this cold creature, its many heads behind the one same-same mask, a singularly-minded *DEATHLY BEAST* hell-bent upon naught but the destruction of all things good and pure with a vicious malicious contempt unleashed against, not just England, or the world in full, but against sense and reason and just plain hardy and ever faithful, English good form first and foremost.

Via *BLITZKRIEG* the German would have his day, but not the night, nor the day after or any day from that moment on, for from that moment on, all, though it took, time naturally, for such declarations of war to reach the eyes and the ears and hearts, minds, body and soul of every man, woman, and child alive in these times, especially in England, now that England was at war with Germany, and more to the point, we were at war with that *HIDDEN HAND* in the grip of which, the strings of this puppet Germany in full.

DARK WEB of an imaginary **SPIDER**.

As yet **THE WEB** still spins, somebody somewhere, in my time and in your time, serving such as this **OLD MAGIC** hidden behind the seams and flourishing in the shade of this **DARK VINE** least in The Light of day, these unhallowed eyes and the fruits of this preternatural wickedness be seen for **THE WOLF** they are, and **THE WOLF** it is, regardless of that sheep's clothing this **WOLF** wears like it be their naked flesh: The fruits thereof, naught but **DEATH** and **DESTRUCTION** and **DECEIT** and **DECEPTION** and **DECAY** and **DECADENCE** and **DESIRE** for all that is unwholesome, and ultimately, **DARKNESS** as the lights go out all over the world never to be lit again.

As faced we, so face thee.

Be warned. Be wise. Be wary. Only Germany was defeated, only Germany was brought so low as to be put on its knees, though 'twas not made to kneel as we but severed the secret strings that tethered this great Nation to **THE HIDDEN HAND**. Nor was, with Germany's defeat this **HIDDEN HAND** severed from the arm thereof the body thereof the head of **THE BEAST** itself.

THE LAPERION that had their day and got paid their due, for having had the gall to try for the world once more, under the guise of a new face and faux fiendish front man entirely, **THE NAZI**.

A day-walking **DARKNESS** indeed!

A day-walking **DARKNESS** indeed!

A day-walking **DARKNESS** indeed! This otherworldly **EVIL**.

As in your day, never was it more obvious than it was in my day, seeing as, it was in my day that this long *HIDDEN WICKEDNESS*, finally took to a more open-world stage so as to tread the boards, before that curtain fall they brought down upon themselves, as *THE NAZI*.

As in my day, so too in yours!

Fear not this *BEAST* though, such as would make a waste ground of your heart and a vast emptiness of your head. Shore up thy Soul with thy Spirit and thy Spirit with thy Soul, for you are a Wizard my child, and never in The Worlds that exist beyond the seams and dreams of your own without measure for thy Soul's eternal pleasure, was there ever a more Magical thing in The Worlds than that!

Be not sheep asleep nor sheep awake, nor *WOLF*, nor ought that ought to fall in-between, and never be thee shepherd, for shepherds keep sheep and such as *WOLVES* in their employ to keep such as their sheep inline, or at least, within those paddocks behind those imaginary fences such as *SHEPHERDS* would have their every single sheep, bar none, no pun intended, believing in the true reality thereof.

Truth is, you're Magical.

And Magical is The Truth.

Beauty is a Fountain: Think like a Mountain.

Run wild, run free, learn to love.

Old Magic is love.

I fell in love, it was the 21st of May, 1940. And it was flight and with flying I fell so truly madly deeply in love with, but then again, this being my first true love in my life, my second was still a few months from finally both crossing my path and making my acquaintance, with naught but a smile I caught like that initial first kiss via this first meeting we were denied, until the very night of the dance, technically, Royal Magical Air Force twice-monthly Ball, 10th July 1940, where gathered once and for all, and for all that were there, just that one last time, our all, every man and woman whose souls, since day one, had been set adrift and sailing upon that good-ship, albeit sky-boat, RAF Skysong, regardless of rank and regardless of regiment.

My sweet darling Jennifer-Jane Songbird: No relation. The voice in my head. The angel on my shoulder. CODENAME: The Dove; herself being one of the girls, albeit ladies, technically iconoclasts, of THE WAR ROOM, RAF Skysong, manor house, it's specific Summer County as TOP SECRET in your day, as it was found to be in mine, least thee, find oneself born with such eyes as eyes capable of seeing, such idyllic, secret and hidden secreted away, Magical & Enchanted and sometimes, Otherworldly things as this?

I was returned to RAF Skysong by Group Captain Peregrine Falcon, via the Mosquito he'd been assigned for this duty: His Mission; bring me back alive, upon the 21st of May, 1940. And such as that, that day in my life, halfway through the greatest summer of my life, to thus start my life, my new life, and such as you might well call my war-story, as an Officer Cadet in training, based out of RAF Skysong itself.

I was even assigned my very own room within The Manor, plus a better fitting, far more becoming an Officer and a gentleman in training, uniform. And thus was my training as a Wizard and a Magician and a Sorcerer and a Sky Pilot begun. All was sky practice. All was sky training. All was flight.

Sleep. Eat. Fly. Sleep. Eat. Fly. Sleep. Eat. Fly.

I was Officer Cadet Arthur Bird, and I gave my life so might you be wherever it is you are, currently reading this story in English, and not, as it might have been otherwise, in German, and yet, be that the case, you wouldn't actually be reading this story at all, for had you found yourself born into an England that no longer speaks English, but German, this story you hold in your hands wouldn't even exist in the first place.

You should take great stock in the fact, that it does!

You should take great stock in the fact, that so do you!

A fractal beauty forever beautiful, beautiful, beautiful, ad infinitum: Shy of liberty ever losing its light.

Freedom can be forever, when thy heart's as light as a feather. Fly, even if you can only fly in your dreams: Fly. Spread the wings of thy mind and soar for naught but the rarefied heights of true reality await you, such has long-waited to hear thy inner bird's sweet morning song, singing in the day anew.

Believe, in Miracles.

For you are a Miracle of a Miracle of a Miracle, ad infinitum, and all the way back to the first Magic, that is in itself, a very Old Magic indeed. The Magic from which, thee did give birth to thyself with thine own song, long before even the stars were afforded their forever stations in the night sky above thy dreams of mortal things and more. Oh is there ever so much more and more and more without end and forever, so says the mystery that is life, forever and ever and ever without end. Not a praying man, nor ever a praying man, I would say to thee learn to dream first and foremost instead, for then, and only then, just maybe, you might just get a glimpse of that light mankind has been praying to since the dawn of *THE DARKNESS* come.

Remember: *THE DARKNESS* has already had its day.

Live therefore in the light of thy own inner self-illumination, and always beware *WOLVES* in sheep's clothing.

Remember: Behind every *WOLF* there is a *SHEPHERD*.

So say the sheep! So says the clouds. So says the sky.

So says sense. So says reason.

So says the light.

Lest thee has forgotten that debt thee owes as thy birthright's due, to all those, who with their deaths, left behind with their crossing over, life and liberty and freedom forever, just for the life of you. For though, once upon a time, a *GREAT EVIL* tried with sticks and stones to break our bones, we never for the sake of you, yielded our dreams in the face of this once upon a time, living breathing waking-world, day after day after day, twenty-four seven, three hundred and sixty-five days a year, courageously endured, in the face of all adversity and overwhelming odds, *NIGHTMARE*.

Upon the back of our great sacrifice, it falls to you to keep *The Dream* alive.

Don't be a patsy: Never think like a *NAZI*.

For puppet **WOLVES IN SHEEP'S CLOTHING** they were.

Puppet **WOLVES IN SHEEP'S** clothing *they still are.*

Lambs become Lions! Let loose the English roar. Cry havoc, and find the bones and stones to say a *NAZI* is a *NAZI* and so start pointing thy finger.

You'll never live in Heaven be thy bread leaven.

Remember, when you remember these days of lore and legend, such as you ought to say of in thy heart, were my days and my time alive in the world, not every *NAZI* was a German, and not every German was a *NAZI*.

Certainly, not every Englishman is an Englishman.

Nor is every American a true American, who loves only life and liberty and believes in that freedom won by this great Nation's many braves. **THE GREAT AMERICAN EVIL** as hidden as it is in your day, as it was in mine, and yet, be that so and be that never truer nor never more in need of being said, again and again, and be thee repeating it, having heard it first said by another, take up this torch and hold it high and hold it mighty, thy good-self speaking with the greater conviction, as rolls this stone gathering exponentially upon its indivisible undividable united shell, the green-green grass of homegrown defiance: It is also as true in your day, as it was in mine, that, that simple Ages old adage thus designed, by design, and Divine observation, and intervention of sense and reason over **MADNESS**, is as I have said, as true in your days as it was in my day.

By their works ye shall know them!

The good, the bad, the even worse, and **THE NAZI**.

Men once, and human, who allowed their hearts and their heads, regardless of which fell first, to that evil that has always been there, and perhaps forever will be, walking down through The Ages with us as may be. But, that said, it is entirely up to you whether or not you walk hand-in-hand or even side-by-side in accord and step with **THE DANCE OF THIS BEAST**, or in saying a **BEAST** is a **BEAST**, and not to be let amongst the sheep, like a fox amongst the chickens, or cat amongst the pigeons, in so identifying this **BEAST** by its works, afford it not the light of thy day; least thy day finally be turned once and for all time finally over to **THE DARKNESS**, as seems this **PRETERNATURAL SUPERNATURAL BEAST'S** sole **DESIRE**.

It is the enemy of everyone and everything this **CREATURE**.

It takes on many names, for it has many faces and followers this **EVIL**, but it will never be as immortal and forever as thee. Yours is the power and the glory, to be, and in being, see thyself as both-

Miracle & Magical.

Lest thy mind be too mundane a mind to comprehend such things as Magic & Miracles, and Magicians, Sorcerers, Wizards and such things of an otherwise Otherworldly Enchanted ilk?

I for my part, as of 21st May 1940, received for my

instruction in the heirs and graces expected of me, if you'll excuse the pun, a crash course in excellence, for I became, soon enough and sure enough, a fully feathered and wing-affiliated Spell-fire and hymn-stone hell-for-leather stones bones and all, pilot of The Royal Magical Air Force based out of RAF Skysong, though that's not to say I didn't see for my part in our part in this war, other Magical Airfields, from Castle Goddard to The Lady of The Lake, which was a pub, and such secret things, albeit places like palaces, that were themselves The Secret Covens of The White Witches of England; such as it was discovered had mastery over the very clouds themselves, for always such as England's clouds answered their call to arms and cover for those innocent souls below, such as these conjured clouds in broad-daylight, shielded from the bombers above.

Wave after wave after wave of bombers sent against our sky! By their Magic combated and confused.

I flew runs to and from these Secret Covens and those Secret Places of The Witch, and of The Wizard, and of The Sorcerer, and of The Magician wherever in England, Scotland, Ireland or Wales such Secrets as these were discovered by me to have been stowed away, out of sight and out of mind of the more mundane world that saw these places not. But as Magic knows Magic and I'd already found my own Magic much became me, and guided by my own inner Magical moral compass, I never missed a drop, or a pickup or a drop off, not once, not in all of the TOP SECRET flights I flew against naught but the sky, battling only ever the direction of the wind, as ever we waited, and waited, and waited, for our enemy to finally bring the storm.

I patrolled the sky in search of those enemy WIZARDS whose MAGIC denied our radar any purchase upon them, but always we returned having failed to make a kill or any kill at all of any kind, for as yet, the enemy was not come. At least, not the enemy we were waiting for. The more mundane less Magical but no less magical all things considered, and all things being equal, be a Man a Magician or not, or what-not or whatever, Royal Air Force, certainly kept the more mundane **Luftwaffe** occupied as we searched the sky not for these mundane souls our radars pin-pointed the positions of so precisely, The Royal Air Force had no trouble finding and fighting these fiends.

On the contrary, our lot was to throw in with their lot.

Magic knowing Magic: True Story.

It was England's assorted Wizards, versus THE GERMAN DEVILS, who were DARK WIZARDS and BLACK MAGICIANS indeed, who came at us, or at least will come at us when finally we come to it, in the guise of CROW and RAVEN and BLACKBIRD and GRAVE-BIRD and DRAGON, behind whose MAGIC DARKLY were the more common flying machines of THE MAGICAL LUFTWAFFE.

The **Messerschmitt**, of which we destroyed hundreds.

The **Stuka**, of which we destroyed hundreds.

The **Dornier**, of which we destroyed hundreds.

The **Heinkel**, of which we destroyed hundreds.

And the **Junker**, of which we destroyed hundreds.

And we fought them all in whatever MAGICAL guise these

flying machines presented themselves as before us, all par for the caliber of whatever *WIZARD* or *WIZARDS* were on-board these machines we rendered onto naught but deathtraps for all those *FOUL SOULS* involved, in whatever form of a fully function thing they sported with a dark glee, such as these things ever seemed want to exude. *THE CROW, THE RAVEN, THE BLACKBIRD, THE GRAVE BIRD, THE DRAGON, THE VAMPIRE BAT,* which, like their *DRAGON,* was a terrible thing bar only their *BANSHEE,* for nothing they sent against us, was as terrifying as their *BANSHEE.* And every beastly flying machine, sang in the sky with their very own song, as did their make believe bullets, and rockets, and belly-mounted or wing-clasped bombs, so might your heart know, just what manner of a beastly thing it was this time, preying upon thy soul in the sky.

Perhaps we'll die?

These were their words, be their machines their sticks and their stones.

A thousand enemy *WIZARDS* slain, and more, surely more. Given, for *that all* they tried to take from us, we gave back plenty, and more! We all chalked up our kills as that War Room following our progress did the same, plotting our positions in the sky via extraordinary Magical and Enchanted means. Certainly, if anyone one or more of us were airborne at any given moment, someone back at The Nest would be following their progress attentively. For I assure you, were I to make mention of that Magic I was to learn was within The Manor House being utilized to astoundingly extraordinary effect, before, all par for my own linear inevitable discovery of this Magic, such as seemed onto my wits that thought themselves previously anchored earnestly to a world I thought I had made all the sense out of that there was to be made, via seeing what I saw, all those things and more that she showed me, I came to know then, that which has never left me since; though I thought myself a wise man of the world at the time, given I was after all seventeen years old, and I'd already had some thirteen or so years already to consider it, give or take, I came to understand I was not a worldly-wise man at all. Never more so imbued with anything but a sense of my own mortality, I had no concept of the abstract concept of death, nor that I, at having reached the age of seventeen so as to become a man, would never live to be any more of the man than I was, at seventeen. For though I couldn't possibly know it at the time, nor even suspect that this might be the case I wouldn't live to see, I'd never in this life see eighteen years of age.

But at least I got to see behind the veil, those scenes behind the backdrop and seams of all that was going on behind our very backs at Skysong, given our ranks and that need to know afforded us and everyone, from the top of the ladder to the grassroots this ladder stands upright upon. Just stood there, like a thing with Magical balance, leaning against naught, as it stands there towering towards naught but a wide Sargasso sky. Such is the chain of command, given all think themselves upon the same damn ladder, when truly, the damned rankers get their own, and those Lords and Knights and Serving Secretaries of The Realm stand upon ladders upon ladders supported by and leaning upon ladders, so might they aspire to a much more rarefied air, and height.

I though, flew higher than they ever could've, or would've, or should've if only they heard the call too. The call I heard. The call I followed. Like a bread trail laid, to be followed, like a bird might peck at ground seed, from seed to seed to Skysong.

Skysong Manor, home of Lord Skysong, was within its old England's walls, a world within a world within a world ad infinitum, a never ending rabbit hole to wonders beyond the mundane mind set. Fortunately, I was a Wizard. And so was she.

For never in a single dream...

Could I ever have imagined...

Such *Magic* & *Miracles*.

Destroyed implying we shot them down and we shot them dead, almost every single day, across all twenty-four hours thereof, the entirety of that stretch that places just out of reach, that victory they had entered our sky presumably assuming would be theirs within a single day and night's misfortune for England, and thus The World in full forever more. But night after night, and daylight attack runs after daylight attack runs, and ultimately back to the night, we fought them off, these **WOLVES** amongst our clouds, preying upon our skies like such as our English sky might be naught but the exclusive hunting grounds of these **WOLVES** and their flying machines and their **MAGIC BLACK**.

Only once did I ever see at a distance Air Chief Marshal

Lord Dowding upon one of his under the radar visits to RAF Skysong, he who was Royal Air Force, whereas myself and everyone else but he upon our base, was Royal Magical Air Force: Of this man I will say only this, though in the mundane world of mundane things and mundane minds, his actions and reactions seemed to make little sense to such as couldn't fathom both this man, nor his actions, and by comparison, his every inaction, he worked in accord and tandem with England's Wizards to keep the sky over England, naught but a promontory of our own orchestrated music, such as the birds of Britain call sky song.

We fought *THE WIZARDS*.

And their *WIZARDS* fought back, with *MAGIC* and *BLACK*.

He fought their winged-sheep, those flying lambs for lions that were sent to their slaughter, for all that came, we killed, and killed, and killed, until they just stopped coming to be killed any more, and so it was come; finally, after ten thousand hours, The Battle of Britain was done: The Battle of Britain was won.

By the few, the brave. By The Royal Air Forces of England, be they Magical, be they not: Heroes and Legends they were, regardless of how long, as in Dowding's most unusual case, it took their Country to remember; Dowding being a first without equal, to actually be forgotten prior to the ghost of this man returning for his due.

It took The Wizards of WWII, and all those who lived never to speak of The Battle of Britain again, to remember him, like Marlborough, like Nelson, like Wellington, Lord Dowding.

Though one wonders now if Churchill himself was thinking of this man when he immortalized himself, and not the man, when he said- "Never in the field of human conflict was so much owed by so many to so few."

But then again, he only said this after The Magical Air Marshal did himself say, in rousing address and somber sentiment before all those Wizards who survived the affray, all of whom he gathered together when 'twas finally done, his every Officer of every rank, and all from The Nest and all of the ground crews of every hardy headstrong rank and file, auxiliary Magicians and Officer-class Pilots, who were, though they were Officers of The Royal Magical Air Force, they were first and foremost, gentlemen. Men whose like the world may never see again- "Never in the field of Magical conflict was so much owed by so many sleeping Magicians, to so few Dragons."

Though here, now, from your point of view, is there, then, remember, lest thee forget, the ghosts of The Battle of Britain are flying even now, for clouds can be Spitfires, come rain, sleet, or snow, given for ever, 'tis naught but their ghosts for whom the wind does still sometimes blow. I could name them all, but that would not pay these men their due.

I can still see their faces, but that alone does not pay these men their due.

I could chisel their names and their likenesses into stone for all time, but not even that could ever pay these men their due. For they were Wizards, and they were Warriors, and once upon a time, they were Heroes. And not but for dying do I say such as this lightly. For be they dead or be they still living when all of this was finally done with, Heroes they were, every man, woman, and child that served such as The Magic of England, and heroes every man, woman, and child that served other English things, being not themselves, folks of a Magical ilk, per se.

R.I.P

The Battle of Britain

10th July 1940 – 31st October 1940

'Per Ardua ad Astra'

All was, at least during May 1940, June 1940, and July 1940, seemingly one long endless Summer that made thy days halcyon. I flew choice dispatch that couldn't be broadcast even over our Magical channels, and picked up secret packages and delivered secret packages from secret places to places so secret, even in saying what I have said of these places, I have already said too much, but then again, I'm dead so what does it matter?

And every single evensong we gathered under the boughs

of the trees, sitting upon our dark canvass deckchairs, drinking wine, eating cheese, sitting in the light of those bough-strung fairy lanterns, a real life Fairy in each one, the Fairies having stepped up their own war footing and war readiness all par for our war effort, that was their war effort too, along with all manner of Magical previously-presumed Mythical imaginary Enchanted things, the likes of which, would dazzle you dizzy and fill thy dreams with naught but fanciful notions forever more were I to name for you but a single one.

Those were the days, albeit the nights of those days of halcyon. Those nights we spent listening to English free radio and those songs you would call old classics or the songs of yesteryear be such songs as the songs we heard and danced to not to thy tastes, or thy temperament, but to us, were as cutting edge as it got and as entertaining for the most part, as any song ever was. Be it the latest George Formby, Vera Lynne, Glenn Miller & His Orchestra, or Grace Fields or The Ink Spots or a hundred and one other contemporary artists, or just The War Report, for never was there a more cutting edge broadcast as that, not that you could ever dance to its tune, least thee be a Fairy.

The Royal Magical Air Force taught me how to fly, but it was the twice monthly All Airfield Attendants Ball that taught me how to dance, the steps of which I took to like a swan once a certain damsel of a dame from The War Room caught my eye, but not I hers until the night of July 10th, which was a Wednesday in case you're wondering. My angel.

Before that fateful night though, the things I had both seen and done, London from the air both during the day and at night, before the blackouts hid the ground from the sky and made such as the sky seem like the ground given in this darkness, no distinction could be made between the one or the other, short of the moon showing one the way.

I'd flown under the clouds and over the clouds, and in all kinds of weather despite this summer's scorch and clear blue serenity that ever serenaded our daylight missions with an illumined reassurance that upon our wings and our prayers, though never a praying man myself, all of our dreams could come true, if we just dared reach out and grasp them, for dreams being dreams, and Enchanted things of an otherwise Otherworldly ilk, 'tis the dream that latches onto thee, long before thee has the sense to wake up to it, and notice thy dream already has thee in its clutches.

Carp Diem.

I seized both the day and the night and every single opportunity The Royal Magical Air Force afforded me, once I'd earned my wings with them, to fly and so rack up more hours in the cockpit and more tricks up my sleeve. Myself being new to both The Royal Magical Air Force, such as I was told had once been known as The Royal Magical Flying Corps since its creation in 1912.

I flew like I was drifting amongst the stars upon those nights filled with stars, or clouds be the night filled with cloud, or rain be it raining, and lightning and thunder and all kinds of winds and weather and clear blue cerulean skies that made such as the green-green grass of the land never seem greener than it did on those days through which I soared. It took me all of a day to learn why this airfield needed no refueling tanks, nor vast reserves of ammunition and belly bombs, for all via that Magic each and every Wizard had learned how to harness, all was Magic and Make Believe.

We made believe we could fly forever, and upon some days and nights it was like we did.

We made believe our own Magical bullets, for we were already assured our enemy's WIZARDS were doing the same. Magic bullets, the cutting edge thereof, imbued with such a bite, like Magical tracers these colorful wisps of things, like ballistic projectile fireflies that lead many an ENEMY BEAST to burn.

We even made believe our bombs.

And we made believe we could live forever, though for some of us, if not many of us and more, such dreams in this lifetime, because of this WAR, alas did not come true for everyone, be they Man, Fairy, or Mythical Magical thing of an otherwise Otherworldly Enchanted ilk. All creatures great and small, all paid the price for this WAR and that part they played within it. All being in it to win in from the beginning. Such as fought alongside the Army and the Navy, and as you've probably no doubt guessed by now, The Royal Magical Air Force, and me.

I flew every single plane, but always thy bird remained thy bird, regardless of what plane I was aboard, just as long as I was the pilot. When I joined other Wizards aboard those extraordinary flying machines that boasted sometimes as many as eight or nine or ten or eleven or even twelve Wizards, we between our grasp of Magic, and Miracles, manifested, other extraordinary things.

We patrolled the sky over England.

That was our duty. That was the job that was our job to do. Always on guard, and ever able to answer to the call to arms be there idle birds upon the ground within three minutes flat; least all Squadrons already be airborne. In which case, in being unable to ever be in two places at the same time, all came down to the fates and the fortunes of the few, that eventually, with the true onset of the first great aerial conflagration the world had seen for many Ages of Man, became with each passing day, fewer and fewer and fewer.

They lost ten and more at least for our every single one, but always that one, in being someone, and not just anyone but someone we both knew the name and makings of the manner thereof, these silenced souls lost to the seas of the sky, 'twas a loss we all both wore and bore heavily.

At night we looked for these brothers amongst the stars, or during the day amongst the whispers of the winds for whom such as these winds of change and transformation once blew. None came back though: Per Ardua ad Astra.

Through Struggles To The Stars.

None came back, but for my brother.

Claude came back first I should say: Least that was just thin own Make Believe just playing tricks upon thy mind? My brother, the ghost of my conscience, and my fortified courage, conviction, and my every curtesy conjured for whomever, given I knew as they knew, but for a simple twist of fate, we may never live to look each other in the eyes again.

WAR being WAR and this WAR, brought upon us by MADNESS!

And here, having thus finally mentioned this one simple inalienable fact at this point in thy tale, I must now take thy mind back, as I take mine own mind back with thee, to that night that was the first night, Claude made his ghostly presence, in such a ghostly form as he walked the world yet, in his pyjamas, known to me, so might he hereafter be just as familiar to me, as was I a familiar to him.

It was the very dawn of the morn I was asked to choose for myself, just which manner and model of a flying machine I would, with this choice, choose to make thine own. For though I was not myself a Dragon, in being that bird that I turned out to be, placing my good self for the duration of my life, but for a singular bombing run I made aboard a Seagull over an enemy COVEN hidden in the French Alps, it made no sense to our collective war effort at all, to afford me anything but my choice of single seater fighter planes.

I was walked to the airfield upon this morn by my Flight Lieutenant, a Wizard called Spellcashier, who informed me mid-stroll I was no longer an Officer Cadet, but would be from that moment on, and from my very next mid-stride, and until the end of my part in this war, a fully-fledged, having been taught how to fly, Pilot Officer.

I could have chosen my very own Spitfire.

I could have chosen any flying machine I wanted.

Supermarine Spitfire, Bristol Blenheim, Bristol Beaufighter, Bolton Paul Defiant, Gloucester Gladiator, Westland Lysander, Lancaster Bomber, Vickers Wellington, Fairey Battle. All of these planes sat idle upon the airfield upon this misty morning, it being 1st July 1940, Monday, 06:40 AM.

Most Wizards favoring first and foremost, a Merlin engine, I chose that plane, within the mist, beside the landing gear of which, was stood my brother's ghost. A Mosquito. A two seater plane I would never actually fly with anyone but my own brother's ghost sitting pillion and passenger so to speak, the rear dorsal-fin-facing machine gun ever in his hands as his eyes searched the sky in my wake for something to decimate with his make believe imaginary ghostly bullets, the tracers of which were a brilliant white hot glowing spark.

'There,' I told my Flight Lieutenant. 'The Mosquito.'

'Brand new Spitfire right there waiting for you Officer Bird,' he told me, even going so far as to point it out for me just in case I'd missed it amongst all of those idle planes only just now being attended to by the early risers of this morning's shift of ground crew.

'Yes sir. But no sir. The Mosquito.'

'As you wish,' he told me. 'I'll update The War Room.'

'As you say sir. Much obliged sir.'

'We'll I'll leave you to become acquainted with your warbird Officer Bird. I'll be in the Officer's mess, finishing my morning coffee.' That said, he left me, just as he'd suggested, to both acquaint myself with the Mosquito, and reacquaint myself with my brother's ghost, such as it seemed I could see and he could not. But when I reached my Mosquito, it was like he'd never actually been stood there in the first place, for such as this I discerned the moment I walked from that distance I sighted my brother's ghostly mirage-like form therefrom, up to placing myself for the very first time, up close and personal with my very own Royal Magical Air Force-issue De Havilland D.H.98 Mosquito.

Country of origin: Great Britain.

Crew: Two. 1 Wizard. 1 Ghostly apparition; my brother and I.

Two Merlin engines.

Maximum speed: Make Believe.

Maximum service ceiling: Make Believe.

Four 20mm guns. Ammo count: Infinite.

One 57mm gun. Ammo count: Ghostly.

Under wing rockets. Load: Inexhaustible.

Call Sign: Mocking Bird One.

I walked the grass upon the ground around this flying machine, touching its landing gear and never more so in my life was I ever so thrilled than I was in this pristine perfect immaculately encapsulated moment, born of mist and dreams and otherworldly Enchanted things. Wherefore art thou though thy brother I could not say or even be sure I'd seen what I'd seen, least this lingering mirage of a ghostly apparition naught but that sleep I was not yet upon this misty morning so fully awoken from, both upon account of the early hour, that late night that was just the night previous, and my abstaining upon this morning my obligatory hot cup of black coffee, that I'd left in the Officer's mess the moment word came down the obvious chain of command, today was the day I would be given that fighter plane all thought my due.

What was it they'd said of me?

Ah, that's right: "The most powerful Wizard to walk the world for an Age."

The bird as it turned out, was indeed the word, and word of the bird I turned out to be, ever preceded me, everywhere I went. Everyone knew before I even knew, given, upon account of those events that caused thy inner bird to both reveal and unleashed itself upon a poor unsuspecting lost enemy CROW, and The World of The Wizards in full unfurled splendor and magnificence, and Majesty and sheer Miracle if you ask me, that caused, upon account of those injuries I sustained in this clash of combat, a Forget-Me-Knot Spell to be cast over me, short of my lips in being loose, upon account of that Field Hospital, that in being the closest Field Hospital to RAF Skysong, I ended up within, secrets best kept amongst secret things, might via my own loose lips have been revealed.

Unbelievable as my revelations would have been, or not.

The most powerful Wizard to walk the world for an Age?

As far as I was concerned, that yet remained to be seen, least of all by my eyes, given I still did not fully appreciate or even know for that matter, at least to my own standards, just what it was a Wizard was in the first place. There being I imagine, in your day just as much as there was in mine own days, which are these days, much conjecture and confusion in this regard, concerning just exactly what a Wizard is, and just exactly what a Wizard is not.

Magical being is a Wizard.

Thing is, we're all Wizards. Some of us just don't know it though. Mundane The Wizards call such sleeping Magicians as that, such as breed naught but mundane things and mundane machines, that all if you ask me, had their advent in The Magical World of The Wizards first, from planes and trains, to automobiles and a thousand and one inventions and discoveries and more: From radio to radar to television, from photography that is itself a Magical form of Alchemy, and a product of The Boom Wizards of Ancient Khemit, to the moving Magical still life pictures of the cine-reels that cause like a zoetrope, the Magic and the mundane to walk and dance and appear to be moving upon the screen. I'm sure, even in your time, you can spot these wonderful inventions and things easily enough, especially if such things seem onto thee, Magical?

Inventions and discoveries of an otherwise Otherworldly Enchanted ilk.

Like my DE HAVILLAND MOSQUITO, Merlin engine powered

fighter plane. I was already in love with it. It had me at choose your own flying machine. I did not choose it though any more than it chose me. It was all Claude's doing and choice, and in being his flying machine of choice, it became upon this morn, my only flying machine of choice. Chosen for its two seater capacity though no one had the eyes to see anyone aboard this thing but me. But all heard his voice in their headsets and every pilot that flew alongside me mid-skirmish in the sky with our adversaries, saw my rear machine gun loosing ghostly rounds, and marked those enemy planes this unmanned seat and this unmanned gun decimated spectacularly.

We were Mocking Bird One, and we were Legend!

Pulchritudo est fons. Cogitare sicut a monte.

As it was though, as it is right now in this story, such as I will reset now to the afternoon of the 10th of July, 1940, the sun was in the sky, the clouds were few, and the blue seemed extraordinarily beautiful, and I was grounded: Which was perfect, as this was Wednesday, the day of the Ball and the day that was the day I'd been waiting at least the last two weeks for, if not four weeks but no more. This being a tale of many things I can but suppose now, from this place of relative hindsight, able to look back at those days that were, both the best days, and the last days of my life, I should say, 'tis a boy meets world story.

An adventure story. An action story.

An aerial romance in a time of war story.

A Royal Magical Air Force story.

A story of boy meets flying machine, and flying machine meets boy, for I was not but just seventeen years old, and by far the youngest pilot all of England was counting upon to keep it safe and its skies free of *CARRION*.

A story of boy meets Magic, and Magic comes to know a boy. For surely it is all of the above and so much more, if not a hundred and one things and more. For must I now, upon account of an allowance of wit and word and the telling of my tale both sweetly and deeply, set aside a hundred things and favor over this all, just one thing, I would say, on behalf of that one indivisible inseparable storyline that was, for just one evening, entangled with thine own, I would add, 'tis also a story of boy meets girl, and girl meets boy. For it is into the shoes of this sideline storyline I must now step, so as to place myself, in my shoes, accordingly.

Ready to dance the night away, most likely to Glenn Miller & His Orchestra, when who should it turned out to be, but Vera Lynne herself, twenty-three years old and already the national treasure she would forever live to be, upon this fine crystal clear summer's evening in the year of the war, 1940.

She was my damsel. She was my dame.

My gal. My sweetheart. My sweet English rose. My dream come true. The voice in my head that ended up in my heart. The Fairy tale Princess I attended this night's Ball meaning to woo with a near-singular focus that left no room in my mind, but not my heart, for other things.

Vera Lynne you may ask. But the answer to that question is

no, not Vera Lynne, replace her instead, if you even know who she was despite most likely being unable to place her face to her name, with my War Room rose, Jennifer-Jane Calling-Bird in the flesh. For allow me now to paint for thee, a still life picture in thy mind, of this sweet English rose. Least thee be able, with whatever Magic your mind's eye doth possess, to imbue such as this gal, via the Magical zoetrope of thy mind, with all the graceful style and finesse I found her upon this night, lost in the grip of the clutches thereof, such as beauty incarnate.

She was blonde, and no hair ever to my eyes ever looked blonder. Neither short nor long she wore it in such a style and fashion, I would say of her hairstyle, the lady of the manor, such as all of the girls of The War Room sported, but what with her perfect blonde waves and curls in their updo, ever it seemed more becoming of her in my eyes, than any other dame of a damsel there was, none of whom ever caught my eye like she caught my eye first, my heart strings second, such as she strummed every single time I chance a glimpse of her in passing, and my head next, which she ever seemed to come to fill in full, as I found myself both flying for her, and fighting for her, everything else after all being naught but an abstract concept.

Her lips were bright red, and no lips to my eyes ever looked redder: Hers being the reddest lips in all of Skysong.

Her eyes were blue, and yes, no eyes to my mind had ever seemed bluer than her deep blue eyes, against which, and the beauty inherent therein, I will not now measure against ought as obvious as a cliché; for her eyes were more becoming ought as low as that.

And just as Magic knows Magic, love knows love.

It never occurred to me that, seeing as she was a Wizard too, such as she, both woman and Wizard, might actually already know. It was just shy of dusk and the light of the day was fading, but brightened by those Fairy lanterns golden and glowing with a subdued summer in each six-sided tall glass looking glass lantern. Though usually of an evensong only to be found strung amongst the trees, upon Ball night, these things stretched along the paths all of which lead to Skysong Manor.

On this evening I walked the path alone, having taken the air to better calm my nerves for this was the night, and this would be the Ball, I would finally make her acquaintance. Our eyes would meet across the crowded dance floor, Vera Lynne would be singing her favorite song, and not no one would be so unattended to be free to catch me looking at her and thy dame looking back at me. And then we'd dance, and perhaps, by the end of it all, so might this be the beginning of forever for us, a goodnight kiss?

What dreams would come of that?

Both sweetly and deeply.

All had been planning, and preparation, preparation, preparation, I was prepared for that had been the plan. Prepared for everything but that one thing I wasn't expecting, via whose unseen unravelling of thy plans I did not see coming until I walked straight into it, hitting this unseen unplanned for and unprepared for happenchance of fate.

She was stood outside the manor doors smoking a cigarette alone, all but a femme fatal half stood in the shadows of soft lights behind the doorway itself, and one half a vison of the sublime. I stammered in my stride, thrown by this chance encounter with this dame I knew no better than any other, and losing all of my determination in that one faltering moment, I said nothing and made as if I was just going to walk on by without a word said.

My mind focused upon losing myself swiftly behind the great open doors into the interior of Skysong Manor, I hastened my stride, seeing her out of the corner of my eye hurriedly taking one last drag upon her cigarette before quickly crushing it under the toes of her high heeled shoes, so as to quicken her own quick step to catch me upon The Manor House threshold. With but a single stride I would have been through the doors, but as it played out, she slipped herself beside me and placed her arm around mine own. 'You know that was my third cigarette,' she said. 'But not my first drink.'

'Drink?'

'A half glass of something sweet,' she said. 'I left it upon the wall outside just now.'

'Oh, I see. Would you like me to-'

'I'm Jennifer,' said told me.

'I. I err…'

'It's nice to finally meet you Arthur.'

'Yes. Yes of course. It's a pleasure to meet you too Jennifer-Jane.'

'Why Officer Pilot Arthur Bird, have you been checking up upon me?'

'Yes, I mean no. I mean-'

'Come on shy boy,' she said with a giggle, Vera Lynne singing in the background as she took me by the hand, and skipped off up the great grand staircase with me, leading me I did not know where at this time, but it certainly wasn't in the direction of that great hall set aside for this night's Ball.

Long story short, she secreted me away to The War Room, currently occupied by a few occupied dames too occupied to show any interest in those two giggling lovebirds skipping the sidelines upon only the peripheral edge of their disinterest. No doubt these dames had all done this themselves in the past. From The War Room into more Magical and Enchanted areas filled with all manner of wonderfully inventive means of monitoring the sky and the coast and the channel between England and mainland Europe, and France first and foremost, we slipped for slinking candidly.

She was slightly intoxicated upon her bubbles whereas I found my mind fed by other things, and more Magical things than bubbles, though truly naught but a kind of Magic puts such as bubbles in one's glass. She took me into a large chamber, the floor of which was an living breathing real world moving motion-imbued aerial view over England, and England in full, and the air above this floor was the sky.

I was speechless. She was not. 'It's beautiful isn't it Arthur?'

I didn't have the words. This room quite took every single thing I might have said, not so much out of my mouth, but verily out of my very mind before I could even use it to think of ought worthy to say of such Magic as this.

I'd never seen it's like before. I did not even know such beautiful Magic as this existed anywhere in the world, let alone right here and right now, secreted away within Skysong Manor upon a purely need to know basis entirely. I evidently didn't need to know, but knew now, and forever.

'It won't be long now,' she said, her words leaving such a smile upon her face and never a more so desirable kiss hidden and locked away within the very secret corners of her smile, the key to which, perchance the very sparkle of her eyes alive in these days of halcyon and uncertainty and the greatest unknowing.

'What won't be long?' I asked her, my heart adrift in every single beating moment.

'The night lights of England,' she said. 'And oh, the sunset when seen from this room Arthur.'

'Yes, of course. I'm sure it is quite wonderful.'

'Quite wonderful?' she questioned, mocking my sublimity. 'Oh you silly boy,' she sang with the song of her giggles.

'Yes, sorry. I don't know what's come over me.'

'Kiss me Arthur,' she said, puckering her lips and closing her eyes as it crossed my mind that I might, nay, must have been abed and a-dream, and though in the very next blissful moment, I had been about to taste my very first kiss, the fates and the fortunes or every single man, woman, and child in England denied my heart the purchase of this, one of life's true adolescent joys.

Boy meets girl. Girl kisses boy. Boy falls in love.

But upon this night nor any night in my life, it just wasn't meant to be, war being war. And this war, upon this night on earth, July 10th 1940, finally was come!

The moment I spotted naught but an ominous tiny black speck of a thing, The Map Room accommodated me with a much closer face-to-face look at that patch of offending sky, and both I, and she, were left speechless.

Already the airbase sirens and every man's call to arms was sounding, and not much more than seconds later as it seemed to my depth of perception of these next few moments, The Map Room and The War Room came to life and filled with Officers of every Magical rank and more.

The enemy was come, and had launched against us, the greatest Magical aerial armada the world had ever seen before.

There were hundreds of them!

Maybe even thousands!

BANSHEE and *DRAGON* and *RAVEN*, *BAT*, *CROW*, and *BLACKBIRD* saying bye-bye already to the coastline of France. Squadrons upon whole Squadrons of these terrible war machines, flying in strict disciplinarian formation, stacked Squadron on top of Squadron on top of Squadron, thus seeming to fill the entire sky from rooftop height to the sky's very underside.

All were incoming, as yet twenty miles out from The White

Cliffs of Dover. All were coming! This was it now. This was the war. The entire sky over the channel would soon be filled with all manner of enemy **BEASTS** of a dark black burden indeed.

I don't think my heart ever beat the same way again.

Finally, *The Battle of Britain* was begun.

I found myself outside and running, my mind firing so fast I had no memory of actually leaving The Manor House nor whether or not I bid my gal goodbye, but with more pressing matters literally hammering down upon me, I raced as fast as my feet could convey me, out across the grass to that Mosquito that was, first without equal, my very own fighter plane, and always, potentially, with my every single Magical mission undertaken, my coffin.

8

FLOCKS AWAY!
⊙
OVER DOVER

I knew Claude would already be aboard my De Havilland Mosquito, strapped into my rear gunner's chair, his back to my own as ever we'd flown so far so good, at least, in the fact that I was still alive, though my brother was not; for I was still flesh and he was not. My brother had forged himself instead a body out of other things, skylight and things like dust and sunbeams and my own mind's eye's wild imaginings. So might I see him, like he was actually sat there to be seen.

My brother's ghost.

So might I always know he was right there, in his own flight seat, ever flying my every single Mission right there with me all the way. Be me flying solo in thy two seater, or requisitioned for other seats and duties upon other planes, where oft I was but one Wizard in eight, or more, or less. But never really less.

Claude was my good luck charm.

My patron Saint of faithful flyers.

My mascot. My Miracle. His Magic, my luck.

My brother, Claude Bird, the one who came back from the great beyond, so might he find his way back to me, and keep me safe and himself secret, until such a time, the odds so stacked against me, and my chances of making it remote, he could do no more for me than that great thing he already had.

Proof of life, proof of death.

He was proof of an ever after. Proof positive of an afterlife. He was proof the spirit of our Souls lives on, every single time he too strapped about his immortal bones and ghostly stones, our Mosquito, twin Merlin engines and all. For he, like I, all par for this war and our war effort within it, had also learnt to fly, only that flight school he attended post mortis, and that one I survived the trials and tribulations thereof, couldn't be more Worlds removed the one from the other than they were.

What do you need to know?

This was war so what do you expect?

I climbed up and into my cockpit as fast as I possibly could, and then sat, strapping myself in, donning my flight cap and headphones before flicking a few switches naturally having already slipped into its receptacle, my Royal Magical Air Force military-issue military-grade combat wand.

That was all it ever took to turn my Mosquito, and me, into the greatest Phoenix of a flying machine, and *only* Phoenix

The Royal Magical Air Force had ever seen since their original inception in 1912; though the impetus for the need was born out of necessity in 1899: That which was, The Year of The Wizard, or at least, the year The Wizard finally had his day, and got paid his due: And the enemy of all good, honest, and decent Wizards everywhere, finally, after thousands upon thousands of years of all that was good and honest and pure in our world, enduring the shadow of this DARKNESS INHERENT, but never a DARKNESS APPARENT, finally got served its own just reward, no less than this TIMELESS EVIL was due.

That was 1899.

The Year of The Wizard, and The First Great War of The Wizards, a war that was fought behind the very fragile seams and dreams of the mundane veil, the whole world over. A war so secret, the whispers of which had been silenced by The Great War of 1914-1918 as it turned out, I actually had to die myself to finally learn of this war's ever resounding echoes, that even to your day, resonate and reverberate with the world even still, and hopefully forever.

The War To End All Wars, that didn't end all wars, the world's first true fallout upon account of that which rocked the whole world cradle in 1899 behind the dreams of such as cradles and things, and this war, in itself, very much the fallout from that one: The hidden History of The World, and that of the entire Human Race for that matter, being a thing so entangled and entwined and interwoven with that of The World of The Wizards, and The Magical World in full, it is no wonder Wizards awake call those Wizards asleep, naught but the sheep of an unseen shepherd, who in being so unseen, and not to be seen walking down through The Ages alongside those sheep he keeps, must have been a very powerful **WIZARD**, or **WIZARDS**, indeed.

At least, prior to 1899 and these **DARK MASTERS OF THE WORLD** finding the grip of their claws and talons once sunk so deeply into the very hearts, minds, and souls of their spirit-stricken truth-deprived, truth-denied, truth-starved servitudes, begging and yearning with their every single heartbeat to be free of that **DARKNESS** all could taste the bitter-sweetness of the lies thereof, but none had the eyes to truly see as true as this **DARKNESS** needed to be seen, so might it be seen for what it was, and by its own **WORKS**, and **HIDDEN HAND**, be known.

I was The Phoenix and The Phoenix was me.

A Phoenix.

Never was there a more Magical Beast, and a Fantastical Fantasy Fairy Tale Magic it was born of bar no other dream of a thing ever manifested by a Wizard since Time memorial. I was The Phoenix and The Phoenix was me, and truly we soared as swift as any bird there ever was, be it bird or be it flying machine.

No frame of reference for this Creature of excellence I was able to become, and be, as was it not becoming of me, to be a Phoenix was there in the worlds beyond the obvious simply hand-me-down name of this thing.

Phoenix.

No one had seen one for thousands of years.

And those dusty old drawings, drawn not from living witness nor even as it turned out, living testimony, be that second, third, or even fourth hand the wit of it, all was found to be wildly erroneous in its preconception and driven sense of the fantastical, the references thereto, such as a Phoenix, and the images and illustrations thereof, oft to be found in Ancient and Antiquated Fairy Tale tomes the few of which that I found had actually survived and endured The Ages intact, and not in tatters, and shredded wit and misunderstood word.

Can you see it yet?

Can you see me strapped into my pilot's ejector seat at the very mind's eye of this most Majestic Miracle of a Magical conjuring of one's own inner Totem.

And The Dragons, didn't have a thing on me.

Not that I'd have endured for as long as I did, without them, nor without our all backing up my every single aerial feat of phenomenal aerial prowess and artistry and skill in the field of flying by one's own book, and one's own rules. For this be flight, and when you're flying, no one can tell you what to do.

You fly.

You soar.

You corkscrew, you barrel roll, you loop the loop of via pulling of both this and that aerial feat of excessive luck and bravado, more death-defying aerial maneuvers than that.

The voice all of us heard over our headsets was our Squadron Leader, and his words set the tone for all of us. 'Cry havoc!' he cried. 'And let's slip the dogfighting Dragons of war!'

That said, and without any further to do, I received my clearance from The Nest to launch, and that order confirmed, I took to the sky at the back of those RAF Dragons and Kingfishers, and Birds of a Tropical Paradise and all manner of ornithological Great British bird. Already in the sky ahead of me and already filling the sky behind me, all of our Magical Squadrons took to the air, from our every single Magical airbase and secret Enchanted airfield.

So it was, and soon enough, all bound for Dover, I found myself soaring beside Peregrine Falcons, Robins, Kites, Skylarks, Sparrowhawks, Nightingales, Owls, British Bullfinches, Cormorants, Dartford Warblers, Eider Geese, Firecrests, Goldcrests, Woodpeckers, Hen Harriers, Sparrows, Hawfinches, Jackdaws, Kestrels, and naturally, Merlins.

Hundreds of flying machines manifest and Magical!

Wizards and more in each and every single flying machine this armada of hope and glory and the prayers of all, be they praying folks or not, surely every single man, woman, and child in Britain upon this night, upon hearing the news of this invasion of our sky over the living room wireless, sat before their castle hearths, found it within themselves too surely at least wonder within the very makings of the mechanics of themselves and their minds… Might not The Fairy Tales of our Ancient Past be true after all?

Might they not just be true?

Given to say what I saw of the land beneath me would give too much away where the, even in your day, TOP SECRET location of Skysong Manor is concerned, I will say nothing of it, save to say, where obvious and well-known and much loved landmarks are concerned, no sooner had we reached The White Cliffs of Dover, we were come to it. Lost for locked in a deadly game of it's your time not my time, as we had at every single enemy plane we could line up in our sights, as fast as we could Magically line up this prey, one plane at a time.

I snatched my first confirmed kill out of the sky and into my talons before tearing into and crushing the fuselage of this thing that was both flying machine and **CROW**.

This **CROW** I slung at a much large **Messerschmitt** in the **MAGICAL** guise of an enormous **DRAGON** and thus sent this **DRAGON** spiraling down to its doom below those clouds beneath us. My headset confirmed this kill from The Map Room, relayed to The War Room, relayed to the dames upon the switchboard and thus relayed back to me with the voice of my angel.

"Kill confirmed Mocking Bird One. Happy hunting.'

No sooner was I warned of **RAVENS** upon my tail, Claude machine gunned these two **RAVENS** into disintegrating metal and falling flailing bodies that became naught but an elemental rain of dissipating embers after only a few acres of sky fall in my wake. And all around us, The Battle of Britain, this being the first day's end and early evensong thereof, such as this battle, waged in the sky and all of the sky all around us.

Every which way I looked I saw sky battle.

So majestic a spectacle darkly, all of our Great British Magical Squadrons of many a splendid and varied Enchanted guise of the form of a thing previously naught but a bird, but brought to life by our Wizards and our Magicians and our Sorcerers and those sky pilots of an altogether Otherworldly Enchanted ilk, to surprising spectacle and scenes so sublime, and altogether unwholesome at precisely the same time.

I felt our every loss, whether I knew the man or men in question or not, for they were Wizards and Magicians and Sorcerers and more these men, but first and foremost, they were Englishmen, and it was within England's sky or sometimes within sight of our fair sceptered isle, they died.

Fire-breathing Dragons on both sides, lit up the night and seemingly everywhere I looked, the sky was filled with multi-colored tracer bullets, that although purely make believe imaginary things, these things could maim, murder, and kill in but the blink of an eye that perhaps because of these Magical things, may never blink again.

Spells these bullets. Real life Spells unleashed, made ballistic, presumed projectile, and deadly; as were our sky rockets and as were the enemy's sky rockets, deadly.

And everywhere I looked, I saw rockets.

I saw our rockets wiping out their BEASTS, and I was witness to their beastly rockets wiping out our own. And over the airwaves, everyone was calling out their shots and confirming their kills and calling for help or saying their final goodbyes before these souls were replaced by either static or radio silence.

I saw Chip Wandcaster lost, Bird of Prey and all.

I saw Harry Wand-Buckle, Bird of Prey and all reduced to

naught but noble elements scattering like embers where once a most Fantastical Magical Beast had been.

I saw one of our Seagulls, if not two or three or four or more being ripped apart by DRAGON, and their DRAGON being brought low by our own Fantastical Magical flying machines whose fury was born upon the back of the belly of this battle by sheer necessity and every single pilot and gunner's innermost desire, upon both sides of this epic conflagration no doubt, to make it them, and not thee.

I saw Firecrests glittering as they disappeared amongst embers between the open gates of the clouds, and attack planes burning like streaking meteors that are themselves the sticks and stones of yonder world above the black, where the stars ever hold to their faithful stations, and twinkle-twinkle like diamonds or distant snowflakes that never fall, never settle.

I saw Kingfishers climbing into the flaming heights of the sky and I saw Kingfishers on fire and falling.

Sparrows like streaks blindsided me.

Robins and RED-CRESTED CHASERS, their talons locked as these flying machines spun into pirouettes and impossible maneuvers to break away from without tearing one's flying machine to pieces and scrap parts in the process, for I saw this happening dozens of times for every three or four minutes of battle as it seemed to me.

I saw it befalling Peregrine Falcons, and Robins, and Kites, and Skylarks as flaming and exploding Sparrowhawks drifted into embers, and Nightingales fireballs. Owls and British

Bullfinches and Cormorants I saw flocking and falling apart, and Dartford Warblers taking on **BEASTS** twice or thrice their size. Eider Geese soared high whilst Goldcrests and Woodpeckers soared low disappearing from the blanket cloud beneath this tier of sky and battle. Hen Harriers, and Sparrows and Hawfinches climbed, chasing shadows and flames upon tangents and plains of combat that made of the sky, a cat's cradled.

Jackdaws and Kestrels decimated *and were* decimated right before my eyes, and the Merlin gave their all as from this all, and our all in full, **THE ENEMY** took back plenty.

All of these things and more, haunted me to the day I died, but no longer: Death being the release from such things as you might as well come to know; be there anything even remotely resembling some semblance of a thing of trust between us, and thy truth? Trust me, faithful friend, having read this far and gleamed from thy tale whatever it is you have gleamed, by both design I would hope, and chance occurrence no doubt upon your own knowledge of The Magic you are made of, I was not sent back to tell my tale lightly; lest thee forget.

Because of The Battle of Britain you were born.

Had it gone any other way, rest assured, you wouldn't have been.

Eine kleine Nachtmusik.
Vorsprung Durch Magie.

I could not possibly have imagined in all of my wildest darkest dreams, not that I'd ever had a dark dream in my life before now, prior to waking up to the reality of this **STRICT**

DISCIPLINARIAN NIGHTMARE set and sent against us. Its sole purpose, our absolute and utter total surrender and obedience to THE NAZI.

The living breathing face of THE NIGHTMARE itself.

MAGICIANS and BLACK!

And truth be known, EVER WORSE THINGS than that: Some of these TERRIBLE BEINGS being not even altogether human, or even in themselves from that World we would say of it, our World: Our World and not their World, given the dimensions of this land are the dimensions of our land, and not their land, such as these BEASTS, having been a plague upon their own, have long, like SOUL-SUCKING SOUL-THIRSTY things, had been feeding upon.

Truths I will say naught more thereof, for these truths in being still hidden truths, are truths for other times. Right here, right now, we are fighting for our very lives in the sky over The English Channel, and your mind's eye need not be anywhere else but right here, right now with me.

I watched and listened to the fleeting dispatches over my headphones from Dragon Squadron, picking up upon those accents that identified in my mind, without the need for call signs and code names, just who it was I could both hear and see, despite the differences in Dragon insignia that naturally spelled it out as plain as day. For we weren't all Englishman in this fight for England's skies. We were Polish and American and New Zealanders and Norwegian and Czechoslovakian, Rhodesian, Belgium, Jamaican, Australian, South African, French, Irish, Scottish, Welsh, Newfoundlanders, and then there was the fellow from Barbados.

Colorful characters one and all.

Not all of whom would ever set foot upon English soil again, despite with this fight, somewhere at some point within this fight, giving their life for it.

All for England we fought and we fought for one and every single one of us fought for all, against all that with this battle our common enemy sent against us.

Rorschach painting with black clouds of exploding clouds of burning diesel oil and breathed in inferno living writhing trying to be so might these things be fireballs in the night sky burning brightly, seemingly vying for all but every single inch of empty sky, and I half-fancied I could imagine the giant apparitions of The Magical Air Marshal and other Wizards stood within The Map Room back at Skysong Manor, actually stood there in the world I was fighting for, like clouds, or the ghosts of clouds caught glistening and illuminated by the sky full of tracer fire and flame.

Could they see me like I liked to think I could see them?

Perhaps marking my Phoenix's progress becoming me in this battle for bones and stones and blood and souls, for if ever there reigned with the rain upon any night, a night of the iconoclasts, this was that night, the dusk thereof had seemed so serene and overly-simplified by the innocent promise of perchance a dance, and at the end of the night, our first kiss? Be it a thing stolen sweetly or offered deeply or not.

Spell's Belles I thought, we're certainly dancing in the dark now. I chased a STRICT DISCIPLINARIAN DRAGON through the sky, chasing this BEAST, ever refusing to release this BEAST from my sights as I chased it not for sport, but its kill, be it confirmed or unconfirmed, hearsay, eyewitness account, or what-not or whatever, this DEVIL DEMON BEAST was mine, and I was aiming to kill it, dead.

I would shoot this MONSTER out of the sky if it was the last thing I ever did, and so it was, we embraced this entanglement of fates and fortunes and ever it played ball, rolling and twisting and ever trying to shake me from my pursuit. Oft it thought to lose itself amongst the inferno and the carnage and melees that set their own horizons and planes as fight and fury and fury and fight streamed and streaked upon all tangents and trajectories like flaming strands of the tails of shooting stars and burning Wizards and Magicians and Sorcerers and other things of a more Otherworldly Fairy Tale Enchanted ilk, falling through the sky sometimes with and sometimes without parachutes to come to the immediate needs of their prayers.

On both sides of this aerial conflagration.

Ours. THEIRS.

And still I chased thy DRAGON.

Up-up-up and still it did not get away, so it dived, down through a gauntlet of suicidal fury and mayhem and madness and flowering Rorschach fireballs the petals of which we punched straight through, on our way down, as in straight down, ourselves diving-diving-diving with wild weaving sidewinding maneuvers upon the DRAGON'S part in its plight, all of which I matched magnificently.

We hammered towards an ocean of cloud seemingly on fire itself, like a promontory of imaginary land into which we plunged and so it was, having been fighting above this blanket of total cloud cover we stormed straight through, I came to see that battle for the sky beneath that cloud below that became suddenly the cloud above.

We were over The Channel.

I could see The White Cliffs of Dover.

And I could see those Battleships and other boats and burning flying machines glistening upon the lapping waves getting closer and closer and closer as I chased thy DRAGON down through this second half of the sky. My focus a singular consideration- It will be you tonight!

It never even occurred to me that thy DRAGON might just not pull out of its dive, but such was my focus, I hardly realized I was submerged and flying through a new medium of world entirely as I lined the also submerged DRAGON up in my sights and gave it all those four wing-mounted machine guns had to give, and that was that, it was dead, and sinking down into the dark, poignantly.

To look up, through the waters to the waves above, was to see flames and fire like I'd never seen such things as flame and fire before, and everywhere within the murky depths, dead Wizards and worse were sinking, like their shattered flying machines were sinking, or in just having their backs broken, or a single wing clipped, they kept true to their forms as they sank, both *BEAST* and Battleship, and all manner of Fantastical Magical bird of another Wizard's dreams and inner being and things.

I saw Birds of Tropical Paradises from far faraway, sinking with poignancy in their eyes looking up at the lights as these souls sank down into the dark, and the black, and the cold of The English Channel.

Breaking the surface of the waves, I steadied myself, beating the wings of the bird I was become, hovering thy Phoenix just above the touch of the waves below, as I looked, and I marveled, and low sank my heart.

Battleships were on fire just off the shores of Dover and England in truth, and the waves were lapping naught but burnt and blackened but buoyant bodies, rolling them over and over and over as these dead Wizards and more and worse and less, went wherever the waves on this night deposited them.

And though I couldn't know it, nor ever know such as death taught me, but with thy extended life or at least what was left of it from here on out, be me fated to even survive this very night on earth, when so many of my fellow and much loved and now lost Wizards of The Royal Magical Air Force had not, that fiend that had been thy 𝕯𝖗𝖆𝖌𝖔𝖓, 𝕷𝖚𝖋𝖙𝖜𝖆𝖋𝖋𝖊 𝖕𝖎𝖑𝖔𝖙 𝕺𝖇𝖊𝖗𝖑𝖊𝖚𝖙𝖓𝖆𝖓𝖙 𝕳𝖔𝖗𝖘𝖙 𝖛𝖔𝖓 𝖉𝖊𝖗 𝕲𝖗𝖔𝖊𝖉𝖊𝖓𝖇𝖊𝖗𝖌, a 𝖂𝖎𝖟𝖆𝖗𝖉 and a 𝕹𝖆𝖟𝖎, of the most strict disciplinarian sort, was out there alive even now, floating upon the crests of the waves, kept afloat by his life-preserving inflatable flight jacket, a loaded Luger in his one hand, and his *LUFTWAFFE-ISSUE WAND* in his other.

Not that this wounded fiend would live to cheat fate nor **Der Fährmann** twice, given it was upon a secluded, cliff-face enclosed, small stretch of Whitstable beach, he finally was afforded his due, by children; such as thought themselves having a lovely day out at the seaside, despite one of them murdering in cold-blood this fiend, from which there was no fallout at all: But that is a story for another to tell, least it already be told by such as was there, for only such as was there, a living witness to all that went on, would know the truth of what really happened upon that little slip of enclosed beach, upon which a handful of evacuee children found themselves trapped for a day, with a living-breathing wounded **Nazi** washed up upon the beach with them.

As I hovered there, just above the waves, I marked in the heights of the sky above me, the dying of the final embers of this fight, for 'twas all but dawn and the enemy was done. Those flying machines with **Wizards** alive in their cockpits turned tail and ultimately left our sky be. But even as I watched the remnants of their sky armada disappearing into the distance, I knew, as knew we all, and as would come to realize every man, woman, and child in England, they would be back.

The surviving Seagulls of The Seagull Squadrons descended to hover as I was hovering, just above the waves, dozens of them hung there in the salty sea-crested spray, searching with heightened sense for any man-alive and floating upon The English Channel. Even the enemy, be such as that found alive, was afforded this quarter. For as far as my eyes could see, everywhere upon The English Channel where there were bodies floating face-up and facedown, there hovered, and hung at staggered intervals of the sky as Seagulls came for survivors and left with survivors, the giant Seagulls of Seagull Squadron.

Never had I seen anything like it in my life before: And little could I know at the time, I would never see its' like again; for the next time I would face our common enemy in aerial dogfight and free-for-all sky-skirmish, it would not be above The English Channel, but inland, over England and well within English skies indeed.

9

EATING CROW

(OR)

THE CRAVEN RAVENS

It was not before I was landed, and my feet were once again firmly planted upon Skysong grass, that my mind and my heart and the very being of me, finally took stock and weighed and measured the battle's impact upon thy Soul. I looked at the wand in my hand, that was shaking because my hand was shaking, so I holstered this thing and looked instead upon both of my hands in full, for both of my hands were shaking, and behind all of this, thy mind was rattled.

I looked up, back upon my Mosquito and trained my eyes upon the empty second seat where had sat my brother's gunner Ghost, but he was gone now and had left no physical trace but for his every confirmed kill, that he'd even been sat there in that gunner's seat in the first place. Streaked in soot and oil and blood was this flying machine, that had flown seemingly through Hell itself, and then returned faithfully to its nest. Other pilots were upon their knees I saw, kissing the ground or ripping up from the ground handfuls of grass in despair and dismay. I looked away from these hard-pressed men, thinking I might see my gal, thinking she might have been stood there upon the airfield's edge, waiting for me. But she wasn't. Most likely she was still at her post, her station within Skysong Manor, no doubt guiding further pilots home and back to base as safely and as soundly as she could. My dame and all of the dames back at Skysong Manor likewise most likely.

I did not know it would be some time before I'd see her again. Exhausted, I dragged my sorry weary self from the airfield, staggering as ground crewman like blurs in the corner of my eyes raced passed me, some of them speaking to me in passing, others saying nothing. But whatever it was these few good men said to me upon this morn I did not hear. For I had not the ears for such comments, nor did I favor thy eyes at this time, with which I saw, terrible things.

The dead being lifted down from the bigger birds.

A flaming Albatross crashing and killing all onboard just shy of actually making it back to that runway this Magical thing had been heading for.

A Kingfisher making this runway's start, but not this runway's end.

A Dutch Air Force Dragon, one of its wings broken, struggling to settle down upon the grass.

And everywhere I looked, there was something to see, sometimes terrible, and sometimes hope inspiring. But as it was,

I had not the heart to care to do ought but pick up my feet in some fruitless attempt to both walk away, and put all that was now behind me, behind me.

I could turn my back though, and make believe via some faux sense of let's pretend that it was indeed all behind me now, but I knew that it wasn't. My good heart told me so. For that which was behind me now, with this ongoing war, was also ahead of me at the same time. Same-same again, next time round.

All on the ground at this time seemed a battle.

I walked away.

I drifted aimlessly like a cloud, drawn to that gathering of pilots back from the battle to discover an ad hoc on the run mess cart had been wheeled in, from which coffee and tea and crumpets were being served.

I took a Darjeeling, and a crumpet, watching a single small block of butter melting over the face of this thing and seeping into this crumpet's pores, but I didn't eat it. I couldn't eat. For who could stomach a single morsel having just been force fed a battle it was a Miracle any of us returned from to live to fight same-same, for our skies, over and over and over again, another day, till either death catches up with thee, or the enemy in receiving such a good stern thrashing, simply decides they've had enough first.

Which would come first, for me, for these fellow pilots, as yet remained to be seen.

We all knew we were outnumbered still.

10:1.

I walked to one of the hangars, and finding it deserted, I walked to that deckchair beside the wireless, and sitting myself down, I startled when the wireless switched itself on, and tuned in upon The War Report.

'Not now Claude,' I think I said, and that said, if at all I said anything at all to this empty hangar, I fell asleep with the wireless providing me with a running commentary upon some other sky battle somewhere. A distant thing this fight, or as good as, but still it haunted me and riddled thy dreams with dismay to the point, to wake was to feel like one hadn't actually slept a single wink. If anything, I awoke wearier than I'd been before I'd even sat myself down to sleep, let alone now that I'd actually managed to get some sleep, though how I managed to sleep at all seemed onto my sense of the slumber I supposed I'd found, a miracle.

I dreamt, but these dreams I'll keep to myself.

It had been roughly 07:42 AM when I closed my eyes.

It was precisely 12:01 PM when I opened them. So said The War Report.

I switched off the wireless only to suddenly hear a chorus of disapproval thus forcing upon me the realization that I was not alone any more. I switched it back on, and yet, in doing so, having previously merely switched it off, it came back on, playing English free radio and rather than search the static for a return to The War Report, said chorus of previous disapproval turned swiftly to a collective approval for that station I had found. To Vera Lynn, singing 'We'll meet again', I walked away, out of the hanger and into the sun to see a sky never bluer, cloudless and glorious and beautiful, until I saw the smoldering wrecks and oil-stained pilots and ground crewmen alike, here, there, everywhere I looked. Everyone looked to have been to Hell and back with me, be they pilots or those men upon the ground whose lot was to deal with all we brought back with us, from bullet-hole riddled flying machines, to bullet-hole riddled men.

Men who were Wizards once, but were just dead men now.

There were bodies lying in a row, under ad hoc impromptu torn sheets of tarpaulin, lying as if planted by Mary-Mary Quite Contrary herself, she who had seeded this garden of dead men with all said dead men, lying in row after row after row, absent though of cockleshells and that pretty maid, one to each dead man, weeping for their lost loves.

Hunted down by a young runway steward, a lad of about twelve years of age, he addressed me poorly but keenly as he earnestly advised me- 'Bird sir. You've been given your clearance to take off. Incoming sir. To the south sir.'

I said nothing, and merely turned to see my Mosquito was sat waiting for me. I took a moment. Just a moment. To stand there, my mind empty of ought or anything for a few seconds before I simply drew my wand from its holster, and gripped it keenly a moment before eyeing this thing in my hand.

I turned it around to better see its wording.

IN THE NAME OF THE KING

&

BY ROYAL DECREE & APPOINTMENT TO THE KING

'Happy hunting,' the young lad said to me, for he truly knew no better and I saw that in his eyes this lad was earnest enough.

I thought about it a moment, trying to comprehend just what it was the lad had said to me, or meant with his words, and yet, to consider his words was to realize his words just hadn't found a purchase upon my mind at all, seeing as this words were consumed whole heartedly by my heart instead, for 'twas only upon my heart this lad's words registered, or carried thereto thy heart with them, any weight or meat on the bone at all.

'A message,' I said.

'Come again sir?'

'A message,' I said again. 'Can you get a message to someone for me?'

'Who sir? Where sir?'

'One of the gals in The War Room,' I told him, myself not really thinking straight in these fleeting moments.

'I'm supposed to remain by the runway sir,' the lad told me.

'Very well,' I said to that. 'At ease lad,' I remarked though the lad was already at ease. It was I that had my back up, ridged as it felt, my cockpit already closing in upon me like a coffin I thought, or felt, though I was stood there in the wide yonder open, grass beneath my feet and naught but clear blue skies above my head. With nothing else to be said, and nothing that needed to be said, I walked away and never saw this lad again for he died later that afternoon, trying to save a burning pilot from a burning plane crash, the black smoldering wreck of which had been removed from the field of play long before I ever saw Skysong again.

I took to the sky once more alongside Dragon Squadron, myself the thirteenth bird, climbing high and higher still until we reached a plateau of a sky-plain and via directions from The War Room, relayed to us over our helmet radios, we searched south for those three Squadrons of enemy **CROWS** we'd been scrambled to intercept.

We found them in the sky over Cromley-Babberton, a quaint little enchanted village surrounded by an ocean of harvest fields sunbaked and golden, the town itself an abstract square not much more than a mile and a half along this town's many-sided border. Though it was Thursday, there was a cricket match in progress but this scattered, cricketers and spectators and all as the fight began in earnest and someone sent a **CROW** slamming down straight into the middle of the cricket pitch, and someone a second **CROW** that crashed upon a graveyard just shy of the town's southeastern edge just clipping the church's steeple where spired a slated roof that was itself utterly destroyed.

Above this village we fought a terrible dogfight, trying to draw the enemy **CROW'S** out over the fields but these **CROW'S** just would not take this bait, so it was, above the village and the villagers' heads, our Spitfire Dragons took on the strict disciplinarian CROWS, and literally, despite our foe boasting the greater numbers, we tore that Squadron of CROWS we caught up with apart and let not a single one of them escape our judgement.

I got me three.

Another few shot down five whereas for everyone else, it was just one or two confirmed kills and then it was done. Some few village buildings destroyed and others left burning in the baking sun, we tipped our wings for those children cheering us from the corn fields, and returned to Skysong having been advised a Squadron of assorted Species had already intercepted and seen off the second and the third CROW SQUADRON we'd been scrambled to see off ourselves.

It was 15:32 PM when I landed.

I ate a hearty lunch, and then sat to a deckchair to sleep, at least for a few hours I hoped, but I couldn't sleep, not a wink I was so wired, and so it was, the time 16:58 PM precisely, I was scrambled once more, to fly alongside Kingfisher Squadron as we searched England's sky for an enemy Squadron of RAVENS.

Though they couldn't see me, or us, or any of us for that matter, just as they couldn't see those enemy planes piloted by WIZARDS, we watched from our cockpits a Squadron of non-Magical Royal Air Force Hurricanes crossing our sky heading SSE. 'Happy hunting,' I said to them, speaking into my radio though I knew full well our broadcast channels were not the same as their broadcast channels.

Not much more than a half hour later, we intercepted the enemy Squadron of RAVENS over barren moorland, Dartmoor I thought, upon whose barren harsh heather and tufts of sparse grass, we scattered plenty of enemy RAVENS having knocked these things from their purchase upon the sky without losing to this dogfight and sky affray, a single Dragon.

It was night by the time we were done though, and soaring under a blanket of stars for as far as my eyes could see, we turned for home upon this starry-starry night, the starry nights of which, soon began to blur into just one long night of the soul. Be it night, or be it day, I quite lost track of what day of the week it was, no distinction to be made one day to the next.

Assured prior to going out one day, that it was Saturday, I landed upon Sunday's early hours and ate a hearty breakfast, technically for my, yesterday's lunch, evening meal, and supper all in one just to catch up with myself and that meal I'd missed out upon having been scrambled just the night previous. I ate well. I slept well, but I didn't dream. I had no more dreams left in me I thought, waking to the all planes scramble siren, and that was that. I was airborne within our homegrown hunting grounds once more. It was Sunday, 1900 hrs.

Sunday became Monday became Tuesday Became Wednesday but, though Wednesday it was, there was no Ball. Nor had there been a Ball since the last Ball was interrupted mid-dance by the first day and night of The Battle of Britain. That seemed weeks ago to me now, and was.

I was scrambled, I fought in dogfights, I returned to eat, sleep, and wake up again, just not necessarily in that exclusive order, to be scrambled, to fight in dogfights, to return to sleep and eat and be scrambled again, and again, and again. Every single day, across every single twenty-four hour period, flying sometimes as many as three sorties in a day, but mostly it was just two, and on one day, seven.

Some days as it seemed to me we lost no one.

Other days we seemed to lose many.

I even thought I might have lost my brother's ghost when his side of the cockpit glass and fuselage there and about and around his flight seat was shredded by bullets, in a strafing spray that also clipped one of my wings taking me out of this night's fight in a single moment of furious misfortune for thy flying machine. That was the closest the enemy had come thus far to actually taking me out and down for good, but fortunately I was able to return to Skysong unpursued by any enemy aircraft, where I landed successfully, noticing as I finally set my bird down, my gal, just stood there upon the edge of the runaway, what looked to be a picnic basket sat upon the grass beside her feet.

I had not seen her since the night of the Ball interrupted.

Weeks ago now.

She looked to have seen just as much of the war as I of late I thought when finally I saw her more closely. I could see it in her eyes, the sparkle of which, though diminished, still seemed in my eyes to twinkle. We did not though, upon his starry night picnic beneath the stars as perhaps had been her want, for having exited my plane and made it back down onto the grass, low and behold, it was brought to my attention that I was shot, bleeding, and clearly in need of immediate medical assistance.

I thought I just needed to sleep.

And I did, but first it became necessary to see one gaping gash of a bleeding wound seen to, cleaned, stitched up, and dressed. Sleep though deprived me of this experience and having slept long and deeply, in a dreamless state of No Mind, I woke to find myself invalid within a hospital bed within an obvious field hospital tent.

It was Army from the look of it.

Royal Magical Marine Corp most likely.

There was a nurse, but she wasn't my nurse and was found to have no time for me seeing as she devoted all of her time and her attention to those wounded pilots that required more of her than I could possibly have needed from her.

I was a day getting out of bed, a whole day spent recuperating before I managed to rise, my wound by no means life threatening for I had but taken a bullet clean through the upper meat of one of my legs and that second bullet that tasted thy blood, be it a second bullet and not the final act of the first, merely had grazed my upper right arm.

I had been lucky. Men I knew to laugh alongside, and with, as I had done upon many a jolly evensong some many weeks ago now, and not since, had not been. I did not mourn though, for though there was perhaps the need, I did not see the point mourning these men when soon enough, and before my time I imagined, someone, somewhere, not before long, would be mourning me too.

Having arisen from my hospital bed within the tent, I found my way outside to realize I was currently within one of the disused fields a half mile from the airfields of RAF Skysong and Skysong Manor itself could be seen rising above a near-distant wall of hedgerow and trees. The entire field was filled with tents, dozens of them field hospitals and one or two of them actual surgeries. Thus I had my first taste of a sight of that assistance The Royal Magical Marines were affording RAF Skysong, the Wizards of this Army all wore green and looked just like regular Army but for their insignia that went to great lengths to make a Magical distinction.

Anti-aircraft guns had appeared now I noticed, upon the furthest edge of this field, actually behind a drystone wall, with Skysong situated upon the field between the field-edge of the guns and that field given over now to the Army. It was Nurses mostly, requisitioned from some auxiliary Corp that I could see, some pushing pilots in wheelchairs who would never fly again and others, still nursing yet, men walking upon crutches or stood smoking cigarettes their one bad arm in a sling whilst their good arm, and that hand upon the end thereof, specifically the fingers thereof, still had dexterity enough to sport a woodbine.

It was whilst I was stood there, wondering where my own personal nurse was, or even if I actually had my very own assigned nurse, like all of the other wounded and invalid pilots had been afforded, presumably to better foster a speedier recovery, a pretty face sometimes being all a sick man needs to get him back up and upon his feet. These pretty staff nurses clearly the carrot, such as seemed to me to render all of the wounded men onto naught but donkeys in my mind. Stubborn jackass mules, drawn by these pretty smiles to get back up onto their feet, following their nurses wherever it was these nurses seemed want to lead them. Mostly, it seemed to me, the wounded men had been lured outside for sunshine and smokes, be they the ones smoking, or their nurses, or just those most recent plane wrecks that littered adjacent fields where those planes that almost made it back to Skysong, ended all of their hopes and dreams of seeing Skysong again, in flames in yonder fields.

Turned out my nurse had been given the afternoon off, and this turned out to be for the best, for it afforded my gal, Jennifer-Jane from The War Room an opportunity to catch up with me once more, a fresh picnic hamper in one hand, at least the handle of the basket thereof, and a cigarette smoking in her other.

'Arthur,' she said having come upon me from behind, clad in both sunshine and smile I saw upon marking her approach to me. And *oh* was she ever a sight for suddenly soaring eyes.

I turned, saw her, and my heart performed a barrel roll, for upon this day in my life, and hers, at this time in our lives that was not in itself, the time of our lives, she looked beautiful, because she was. 'Jenny,' I called her, and at this informality she didn't even bat an eyelid. 'You came.'

'Every day,' she told me.

'No one said,' I told her, which was true, no one had told me.

'Well seems to me, at least according to the duty sister, you just got out of bed and walked away, hardly affording anyone any chance to tell you ought about anything, my dashing daring bold sky-pilot.'

'I'm not so dashing.'

'I'm told you both ate Crow and chased off craven Ravens that turned back rather than face your Squadron upon that fateful day.'

'Fateful day?' I questioned.

'The day you came back alive. I was waiting for you.'

'Yes, yes I remember now. You carried a picnic basket I think?'

'As then,' she said, raising that wicker picnic basket in her hand. 'As now- Shall we?'

'Where?'

'Oh I know a spot, a field away. I've already scouted it out for us. We'll be quite out of eyeshot and earshot of Skysong I assure you Arthur, if you don't mind?' she said, and that said, she showed me that spot, secluded and a quiet place away from all common and plain-sight of Skysong upon account of a field's fringe of trees we placed between ourselves and Skysong completely. It was dusk by the time we settled, our picnic obliterated, her rations for the entire month exhausted upon a single sit down upon that blanket she'd brought, picnic fit for The King of England himself I felt. Little more needing to be said between us, we both lay back, my feet facing NNW and her feet SSE with our heads side-by-side, as we lay there for what was left of this night's evensong, just looking up into the stars that on this night on earth, seemed to fill the night sky in full, hardly sparing a slither of a crack between them behind which, the black of this night might be seen.

It was the night we fell asleep together, our heads side-by-side, just lying there upon a thick woolen picnic blanket, like two star-crossed lovers, falling for the stars. The wish I made upon that shooting star I saw, I'll keep to myself though she shared with me her own.

Though she may very well have been a few years my senior, upon this night, the most beautiful night of my life so far, I dared to allow myself the luxury of a dream: A dream I hoped she would be a part of, if by some small slim star-crossed chance, at the very first opportunity, she'd let me be a part of her own?

10

SEAGULL SQUADRON

&
THE SCORCHED SKY POLICY

I awoke alone upon a picnic blanket I'd been left to myself upon, my War Room dame gone, mostly likely back to The War Room and though I would have rather she had awoken me, I understood and appreciated why she had not.

Perhaps she felt I needed sleep?

Perhaps she thought me dreaming and thought better of disturbing such as my dreams when dreams themselves in these times were surely a rarefied thing and as a thing, surely a thing few and far between given all that might befall thee between the one dream and thy next, be there a next? For every single day so far held naught but the promise that there wouldn't be. No dreams no more. No dreams now ever again, if thee be dead.

Every single day, sported that one indivisible inescapable truth: This was war. And every day the prospect of surviving it for but another day, for every single pilot put to sky again and again and again, grew slimmer and slimmer and slimmer with every single sky sortie they flew. For no one could be that lucky forever. It was a Miracle I'd even been this lucky so far, especially when far more experienced pilots, and especially those pilots one thought, as they thought themselves, would live forever, but didn't.

Some didn't even survive day and night one.

Others went on day two, or day three, or day four and more. In fact, barely a day went by over the course of the daylight hours of which, we didn't lose another. It was impossible to put this thought entirely from one's mind, as such, one just had to learn how to either live with it or best cope with it, at least, until it finally dawned thine own time to go too. We all knew we had it coming. We all expected no less. Just as long as we got in one more good innings, and took at least a few more of the ruddy-muddy beggars with us.

This being the end of the night that was, and this the day that now would be, I sat up to the sun and gauged by its height in the sky, it wasn't much past 900 hrs.

She'd left me an apple, a green one, plucked from the adjacent orchard and left upon the picnic basket's closed lid, given it was closed upon naught but an empty basket within which we'd left not even crumbs. Though my arm was still burning, I reneged from actually returning my arm to that sling

I'd sported yesterday, given I'd need my arm if I was to return myself to the airfield-side of this field I'd awoken up within, with a picnic basket in one hand and my other, making good use of that crutch I was stuck with, presuming I actually wanted to be able to walk anywhere upon this day at all.

I made it with the picnic basket as far as that short wall that technically defined the boundaries of Skysong, upon the one side of which there was a crop field, and upon its other, the neatly mown lawns of Skysong Manor's gardens. It struck me as crazy, that even now, in the middle of the war, someone somewhere was still mowing the grass. But then again, it's the little things isn't it, that make us who we are, until such a situation arises that forces us to face up to the truth of just who it is we were in the first place.

War will do that. It can, and it does, and it already had.

War that makes murderers and corpses of us all. At least, those that kill rather than be killed, but as we were killing in the name of The King, and for our Country, even the innocents, of which in war there are none, must surely have been staining their souls with this same blood too. If we were all holding on in quiet desperation, as if this be our own Country's cultural standpoint, you could bank upon thy Soul being worth its weight in gold in Heaven that we were determined to fight them unto the very end of our days, be those days, days of peace bought dearly via our defiance, or be us in such times, still fighting this war we did not start, knew not what offence caused it, but would be damned if ever we were going to bend the knee to ruddy-muddy

Germans.

It was the first mistake made by *THE NAZI* to think we'd ever kowtow to a ruddy-muddy German: We kyboshed that nonsense straight away I thought as such things graced my mind, actually passing themselves off as thoughts that replaced feelings, be they such as that and not instead feelings that replaced thoughts? As it was upon this morn, I forgave myself my wandering mind until it became self-apparent that upon this morn, not no one seemed to be thinking straight.

A disastrous night had by all, whilst I'd slept out beneath the stars, I restored myself to the edge of the Skysong grounds and simply dropped the picnic basket where I stood, cast away my crutch, and walked as best as I could without actually being seen to be pained to do so, so might I be better situated not upon Skysong's garden's edge, but the airfield where the majority of our runways converged.

Something was clearly afoot.

Planes of many distinction were departing on-mass, if not every single plane we actually still had pilots to fly, leaving a dozen or so birds idle upon the grass. I watched them taking to the sky and though by the time I reached Skysong's last idle Spitfire these planes were all miles away, I climbed up and into the cockpit pilot's seat, and began strapping myself in. Without my wand I would not be able to manifest thy Phoenix and without a second seat, I would not see my brother upon this sky-run, but desperate times ever calling for desperate measures, and this very hour seeming our most desperate hour thus far, I donned the pilot's radio set and began performing all of the preflight checks I could think of.

When The War Room advised me I was grounded, I cast off my pilot's helmet and started up the Spitfire. This was my first time in the pilot's seat without my wand, and though this meant I would no longer be invisible to both radar and those non-Magical pilots of The Royal Air Force, who would undoubtedly be encountered somewhere in the sky, I rolled my Spitfire into its starting position.

The runway clear, I throttled forwards and though I'd never had to take off in this manner before, I did so gracefully, full of pride for my own finesse until the first tree at the runway's far end removed from thy Spitfire at least one of its undercarriage runway wheels.

Remembering to retract said landing gear I did so, if only to improve this Spitfire's aerodynamics knowing full well I would not so easily land this plane again. That done, I took to the sky in a high climb that saw me banking round and heading thereafter, South, upon the distant tail end of that Squadron already committed by RAF Skysong to whatever engagement in the clouds, my fellow foolhardy but never braver pilots of The Royal Magical Air Force had soared away upon more wings than prayers, or more prayers than wings, in search of whatever sky-scrap the enemy thus, with their departure, now had coming to them.

My first time in the sky for as long as I could remember without Claude backing me up.

My first time without my wand.

Without my wand crossed my mind. No wand meant no Magical ethereal Phoenix. No wand meant I was flying upon vapors, and what little aviation fuel this Spitfire just so happened to have sloshing around within it. And no wand meant no infinite supply of make believe bullets, which meant I was hammering into inevitable collision with the enemy, completely and totally and helplessly unarmed.

It was no wonder I was being recalled back to Skysong.

I put my helmet back on, and spoke into it- 'This is Mocking Bird one. Please advise a heading. Over.'

'Who the devil is this? Over!' said an unfamiliar voice inside my helmet's headphone without any to do at all. 'Mocking Bird one! Who the devil are you? Where did you just launch from? Over!'

'Ruddy-muddy Spell-fire and hymn-stone man!' I said back into my microphone about a heartbeat before I realized I was not connected now to Skysong, and its dames for damsels in The War Room, but to some ruddy-muddy non-Magical fellow of The Royal Air Force, no doubt in whatever War Room of a mundane Air Command they had of their own.

'Roger, Mocking Bird one. We see you. Over,' said a second unfamiliar voice a few seconds before I spotted a whole Squadron of Royal Air Force Spitfires soaring not quite alongside me given that stretch of sky between us, but we were, at least as it just so turned out, flying in the same direction.

'Consider me along for the flight. And the fight. Over,' I

told my new Wing Captain just as enemy 𝕸𝖊𝖘𝖘𝖊𝖗𝖘𝖈𝖍𝖒𝖎𝖙𝖙'𝖘 and accompanying 𝕾𝖙𝖚𝖐𝖆 were sighted hammering in the heights of the sky towards us.

'This is it boys!' said the voice inside my ears. 'Give 'em Hell!'

It wasn't like it was in The Royal Magical Air Force.

This was more mundane and far less Magical an engagement as I was accustomed to encountering up close and personal enough to sometimes see even the whites of the eyes of thy prey looking right back into the whites of one's own.

So found me, their fury!

So found me, their aces! And so found me, our own!

RAF Spitfires crossed in the sky in-front of me, decimating the mundane enemy that had me in their sights. And it was, at least in my eyes, extraordinarily sublime, a poetry to their finesse, these mundane Spitfires with their non-Magical sleeping Magicians in their pilot's seats, such as knew or understood, for the most part, most likely, nothing of Magic and Wizardry and things of an otherwise Enchanted ilk, but were, despite this obvious home truth, for truly awakened yet these heroes were not, they still in committing their all, gave their all. And for some of them, that last true measure of devotion they afforded their England, went out with the lights in their eyes in sky-scattered embers stretched in flaming dissipating streaks across the sky, and then they were gone.

Our planes and their planes too.

And yet, none went too quietly into the great long night of

the Soul nor left this world without them taking back that plenty these heroes felt themselves due. For they were defending their home skies against aggressive attackers hell-bent on making England's skies, a thing annexed to Germany's own.

'Tally ho!' I heard someone say.

'Tally ho!' I heard someone else say.

As English as fish 'n' chips I thought to myself. I watched in awe of these fellows in their mundane flying machines, and marked, counting, crunching the numbers as we, and I say we lightly for I hardly felt in this fight myself, lost one Spitfire at a ratio of at least one of ours for every ten of theirs. Such was the aerial exactitude and finesse and sublime soar and courageous attack run and glorious death-defying loop, roll, twist, evade, line-up, decimate, move on to thy next target keenly. They gave the enemy no quarter these fellows and performed such bedazzling aerial stunts and maneuvers I was spellbound, left speechless but not senseless regardless of what sense this sky fight actually meant in the greater scheme of things, to the greater scheme of things.

This was my first mundane conflagration: And my last.

I could literally taste their adrenalin at the back of every throat warble these songbirds sang, for they were young, and Spitfire fighter pilots once upon a time. All of whom died before their time, be it before their time and be it not more apt that these hardy headstrong previously immortal young fellows were not themselves born for naught but this glory?

For someone certainly needed to see it done.

Someone certainly was needed to see our sky saved.

All for England.

Lest Scotland, Wales and Ireland ever forget; or The World in full itself: The outcome of The Battle of Britain would, and thus has, defined The World in full, forever more, given, there truly would never have been any taking it back, had our sky been yielded, surrendered, lost, taken, stolen, won via trial by war, and always where war is concerned, to the victor the spoils.

The BLACK SACK that would bag The World in DARKNESS, thy enemy come, till in death do they part with their WARCRAFT. Lambs for lions these German sheep, driven by their unseen WOLVES to bleat for naught but battle. And still it makes no more sense to me now than it did way back then, when, some seventy-seven years ago, I fought and died for my Country, as did they, our enemy, for theirs.

This was war. This was battle.

This was the very battle for sense and the prevailing of reason and liberty for all life, mostly, and The World in full entirely.

Welcome to The Battle of Britain!

Now go kill, or be killed.

Take a number, join the queue. And be thee killed, take some simple solace from the fact that, in being killed, that was one less bullet thy enemy has for someone else. For when your number comes up, your number, comes up.

'Tis a monument now is it not? A thing that once stood alone, but now just stands apart gathering pigeons.

Two planes. Both **Junkers**. I flew through their own dissipating fireballs and rolled into a climb just as a Royal Magical Air Force military-issue, military-grade Magical Decree manifested already inserted into that receptacle added to the common Spitfire to accommodate a Wizard right in front of me. Sent from Skysong I presumed via Magical means, it never once and not for a second ever occurring to me that I might just have materialized this thing myself.

No sooner was this feat of remote Magic accomplished, this thing surely sent to me from Skysong I supposed, given I truly had no depth of insight as yet, into just how deep my own Magic ran. Had I blinked, I might have missed the madness inherent in the transition entirely. I saw suddenly in the sky, not just that Squadron of Royal Air Force Spitfires fighting mundane **Messerschmitt** & **Stuka** & **Dornier** & **Junker**, but a sky suddenly and spontaneously full of Squadrons of Seagulls & Albatross & Cormorant fighting what seemed to me like a sky full of **DRAGONS** the mundane boys of The Royal Air Force did not have the Magical eyes to see, though they could still be shot down by these fiends all the same. And by shot down, I mean torn for being ripped out of their bird's own purchase upon the sky by either talons, claws, or just plain streaking **DRAGON FIRE**.

Some of them were, spectacularly!

Clouds caught fire. Air became embers.

Thoughts became noxious and poison lest thee had no taste for such as that, one's mind too focused upon the kill, for a single death to find so much as a severed string's purchase upon thy heart, when such things were best left unstrung, at least until such a time, as thee finds oneself fortunate enough to be considered one of the lucky few.

The few, the brave, the not dead yet, but maybe tomorrow or the next day or the day for night or night for day after that. For no one was getting out of this alive. The odds were just too stacked against it.

'Mocking Bird one! Mocking Bird one! Engage! Engage!' I heard in my ears, and a Phoenix once more, I banked hard and dove into this fight just as it seemed to me the entire sky for as far as I could see, suddenly caught fire and literally burned, every single square acre thereof, just simply burned!

My cockpit glass blackened, streaked with oil so slick, it ran towards thy Spitfire's rear, clearing my vision so might I see dozens upon dozens of Seagulls burning now!

All was chaos in my ears suddenly! I heard familiar voices known previously for their laughter, suddenly screaming until these voices one by one, silenced in my ears. That was when I realized I was going down too, and there was nothing I could do about it but pull my Spitfire as best as I could out of its dive, so as to glide, dead stick through the air, level with the ground I soared over, until belly first, I put my Spitfire down upon a field whose length was much less than my current speed would require of it.

It was dusk when I regained consciousness to find myself upon my back upon a field, my Spitfire sitting nose down in a ditch that caused it to reach with most of its length back up into the sky like some kind of abstract anti-aircraft cannon, but it wasn't. It was just my Spitfire's ruined fuselage sticking up out of that field's ditch I'd ditched it in. Clearly I'd slammed straight through the cockpit glass and landed upon my back, already out for the count for I found I remembered nothing of this impact that somehow I'd seemingly, and somewhat miraculously at that, found myself at this time able to get up onto my feet and actually walk away from.

I'd crashed alone in a field of my own I noticed now that I was stood upon my feet, though certainly I could see the telltale plumes of smoke burning either black or rising ashen grey from other fields both near and far; smoke that made no distinction be whatever burning wreck one of England's own, or **Germany's**, either Magical or mundane.

It had never occurred to me before to fly with a service revolver at my side, but now, stood here alone upon this England's own field, I considered this an oversight. For just as I had crashed and survived the burn, so too might any number of German pilots, be they mundane, or be they **Magical**.

I would have to be wary, and have my every wise wit about my bones and stones I thought as I stood there, wondering for a moment just where I was, and just which direction it might be back to Skysong, or anywhere for that matter?

To consider that wand I might as well call my wand for the sake of suggesting it belonged to anyone at all, given it was a standard-issue thing; in case of capture, was to find myself suddenly snatching it out of the air upon account of this thing smashing through one of thy previous cockpit's few remaining previously intact panes of cockpit glass, and hurtling, like a ballistic projectile of a thing towards me. Apparently all Wizards at birth are afforded their own Magical Decree, such as seemed onto me, given this thing was a thing of the world of the Wizards, it's mundane world counterpart I would say, was the common birth certificate, with which, and via whose unseen magical corruption, thy parents thus lease out thy life to thy Monarch. Quid pro quo supposedly.

This one, in being common issue did not bear my name, as I was told it would've or should've or could've, be this not a time of a state of war. Apparently, to be shot down in possession of one's own original Decree would thus afford thy enemy thy name and apparently, once appraised of thy name, great burden of pain and torment could thus be exacted upon thee, cruelly.

I looked at it.

IN THE NAME OF THE KING

&

BY ROYAL DECREE & APPOINTMENT TO THE KING

Was The King a *Wizard* I wondered?

Curiously, I really had no inkling whatsoever where the answer to that question was concerned, but seeing as it wasn't a burning question, when the only thing burning at this time in my mind, was my Spitfire, I allowed my mind to blindside this consideration entirely. Best be getting back I told myself, and with this the better burn where my heart and my head were concerned, I gauged an obvious north heading and began to long walk back to Skysong. The day was glorious, mid-afternoon most likely, and the sky blue, the rolling picturesque English countryside green and lush despite this summer's scorch, I wandered aimless beyond a general idea of where I wanted to be, but not so much in regard to where I was.

At least, for all of the seemingly endless miles of uninterrupted countryside I traversed like myself just out for an afternoon ramble, that was, prior to encountering somewhat by chance, the town of Cromley-Babberton.

I recognized the church with the shattered steeple, and that was all it took to place myself, in my mind, precisely in that place I had found myself, back where I'd previously known sky-fight. It seemed upon my approach to its first fallen stones, a ghost town now. Somber the air lingering like a blanket of heavy maudlin and loitering upon the cold cobbles left chilling things I thought upon account of this ghost town's silence.

Where was everyone?

The town proved dead, deserted, abandoned.

'Hello!' I heckled, startling not even birds from trees for though trees there were, birds there were none.

I walked until I heard a kettle whistling, and so was drawn to a quaint country door in a quaint little village cottage, the gate to the footpath to the front door of which creaked, as did said front door, one I found slightly ajar and thus had to better open to afford myself unobstructed passage into the interior of this cottage. Strangely, something told me at the back of my mind, not to make a sound. Claude I thought, for it felt like Claude despite not a word being said between us. Thus, I walked into this cottage's living room slowly, cautiously, not yet sure just what the danger might be, but supposing upon account of a previously never sensed before preternatural instinct, I urged myself not to make a sound.

The kettle on the boil was in the kitchen, that I discovered was deserted despite seeing evidence that someone most recently had been sat at the kitchen table, eating a sandwich and enjoying cheese and crackers from the look of the leftovers. I ate the half sandwich that was left, a few bites, the kettle still whistling behind my back when I noticed something rather odd.

There was a Luger sat upon the kitchen table, seemingly property of no one but the finder I thought, picking it up and cocking it instinctively barely a second before some strict disciplinarian *SS* fighter plane pilot walked back into the kitchen through the backdoor, this fellow having been outside, enjoying the sun most likely in this cottage's quaint little rose bush-aligned back garden.

The fellow had even set himself out a deckchair I discovered, but only after I'd shot this fellow dead without a moment's ado no sooner than had I sighted him, prior to not having sensed this fellow at all.

I took the kettle off the boil and made myself a nice cuppa tea, helped myself to crackers, and walked with my brew out into the back garden. Fellow had really made himself at home I noticed, and so sat myself down into that deckchair he'd previously been sitting in, picked up that old newspaper he'd actually been reading most likely, despite it being in English. It had been left open upon the cricket results.

Fellow must have had an interest I supposed.

Distracted by the sound of disembodied engines in the sky I looked up sharply, and stood up swiftly, losing the newspaper and bone china tea cup and saucer and silver spoon in my haste to better see. Unmistakably I'd heard common Spitfire, and undoubtedly I'd heard mundane 𝕸𝖊𝖘𝖘𝖊𝖗𝖘𝖈𝖍𝖒𝖎𝖙𝖙, and then there they were, clashing in the sky above Cromley-Babberton, just as I had done once upon a time.

I raced back through the cottage, back down its quaint flagstone path, hopping over the gate onto the pavement before I dashed mid-street across the cobbles to stop, and restore my eyes once more to the sky just as a Spitfire passed overhead, barely a few feet of air between us as I seemed to me. The fighter plane chasing it, suddenly strafed by that Spitfire flying suddenly soaring across its path, spun wildly and a split second later, a set of semi-detached cottages disappeared in a fireball as slate and stone and shattered roof timbers exploded furiously.

I ducked, shaken and shocked, and trembling I noticed, until something suddenly came over me, and I found myself charging down the street towards an already ruined townhouse, up the stacked mountain of rubble of which I ran, until having reached its precarious and rugged summit, I reached with the

Luger, and shot at a passing **Messerschmitt** as it pulled out of a dive and thus was sent spiraling wildly as its followed through with the trajectory of its airborne arc and careered off into the heights of the sky, where it exploded.

I watched fragments of this thing's fury raining down over the far outskirts of the town and then realized the sky was silent suddenly. The battle was done. I turned, marking the new desolation exacted upon this quaint little country hamlet of a town, the previous population of which I thought barely a hundred souls, all of whom would have known everyone by name. Supposing it was time to move on, now that I knew precisely which direction Skysong would be found in, I just happened to cast my eyes back to the sky when I spotted a single parachute descending in the sky, that would most likely make landfall upon the southern edge of town.

My Luger already emptied, I looked at it in my hand and wondered, might I not make believe for this gun a bullet, just like I did for the machine guns of whatever flying machine thus armed with machine guns I'd previously known well, the trigger thereof, or at least, thereto. The jeep I heard approaching turned out to be jeeps, and Army, a small detached unit thereof some dozen or so non-Magical Englishman, four to each of the three jeeps they drove through town, clearly having seen the enemy pilot and his parachute, and now baring down upon this thing's exacting landfall position.

The jeeps all stopped mid-street by such stonework and fallen masonry denied their jeep further access to the continuation of buried cobbles, they pulled over, and everyone got out. So I ran, baring down upon the last jeep in the small convoy and snatched myself into this thing's driver's seat, slamming this jeep's driver's side door hard enough to cause that soldier at the back of the wandering unit to suddenly stop, turn around, and just stand there looking back at me.

I looked at him, like a rabbit caught between headlights no doubt in his eyes, and yet, having looked at this fellow looking back at me for a few seconds, the most curious thing suddenly crossed my mind. He said as much himself when he hollered for heckling- 'Sarge! 'Ere Sarge! Another one of those strange inexplicable things just happened again Sarge. Third jeep just vanished Sarge. It's gone sir. Gone. Just up and ruddy-muddy vanished it did Sarge, right before my eyes this time 'n' all I tells yer.'

Well at least that explained that look of surprise I'd caught him wearing I thought, a split second before I started up this jeep's engine, put it in reverse, and bombed back down the cobbles until afforded enough clear cobbles to spin the jeep around, and so drive, eventually with more calm than reckless abandonment, all the way back to Skysong, my brother, Claude Bird, deceased, riding shotgun in his pyjamas beside me the entire way. But then again, no one ever said it wasn't going to be a mad-mad-mad-mad-mad war.

11

"IN THE CLOUDS ABOVE OUR BEACHES."

We drove through the night thus arriving back at Skysong upon the early hours of the morning of the 7th September. 1940. Ourselves arriving barely moments I supposed, just shy of catching a curious stately black car, flying diplomatic flags, make and model of this black magnificent automobile of a machine, a Magical Mystery to me.

The man it delivered to the steps of Skysong Manor, caught upon the steps in the early morning light as we pulled up upon the gravel a few jeep's length from this guest to Skysong Manor itself, technically, where The Royal Magical Air Force was concerned, Strategic Air Command, aka, The Nest, though shrouded himself in mystery, upon account of his backlit silhouette, caught in the early light of this day on earth, with his distinguished shadow, such as cast a likeness of a cigar smoking man, in a black bowler hat and black coat and cane, across the gravel, the man himself could not be mistaken for anyone but the man he was.

The man who was come to Skysong.

Ever he seemed hunched by the weight of the bad news he bore. I watched him turn away from the sunrise upon this morn, and take the remaining steps up to Skysong's threshold, and then through its great stately doors that both opened seemingly of their own accord for this man, and also closed behind him.

That was when I finally realized I was back. I'd made it home alive. Such joy was kindled upon account of the thought that my dear sweet Jennifer-Jane was most likely at her station in The War Room, within Skysong Manor itself, behind those same closed doors, intent upon keeping some lost Soul in a cockpit of his own alive no doubt for as long as she possibly could; or could've, or would've, or should've, if only said pilot's life had been since birth, imbued with such luck, this fate since birth could not possibly have been the fate of this fortunate babe in arms, once cradled in full by The Magical World in life, only to meet head on that Magical World that cradles all Wizards and Magicians and Sorcerers and folks of an otherwise Otherworldly Enchanted ilk, in death.

As it does with Magical and non-Magical magical folk alike.

All wake up eventually. Some in life. Others in death. Some somewhere in-between. For some, never before but in death forever thereafter. For Magic knows Magic always. For Magic has the eyes for nothing else but that.

Hell for those slaves to the root Chakra born.

Heaven for those from whose souls thy Light by The Darkness could not be torn. Here endeth thy lesson in Magic.

Having taken the moment I needed for the moment itself to take, I started up the jeep, and though I'd sped previously at speeds wild and reckless, now I but strolled the jeep quietly upon the gravel until I had grass beneath my wheels, once wings, and quickened my pace to the hangars, this jeep's radio suddenly switching itself on and searching the static for something playing I thought, upon English free radio.

Dozens of planes were idle upon the runways.

About a dozen more had aircrews working upon them under the ad hoc temporary corrugated great arched roofs of the airfield hangars. I saw seemingly every single type of flying machine in our inventory. Some of them brand spanking new and just here hot off the assembly line from the look of these untried and untested birds of prey. Brand new Lancaster Bombers too, and Vickers Lysanders and a whole new Squadron of Fairey Battles. The very dance of the Fairies around these flying machines speaking in volumes where their silent appreciation of the namesake was concerned. Not least of all upon account of the good luck Fairies that flew within them, hoping to bless whatever pilot with their every sprinkle of dusty charm, powering the engines of these specific planes.

For luck, I'd always had my brother's ghost to fall back upon, and though I couldn't actually see him in the passenger seat of the jeep, actually tuning in the radio himself, somehow I just knew that he was there. Something at least had seen me back alive. Something at least had helped keep me alive given all I'd been through since last I was here, just yesterday I thought, or the day before, myself unsure as to just how long it was I'd been absent without any clearance to take to the skies at all, having been grounded.

Only now did I recall thy wounds. Only now did I notice my absence of discomfort and pain of any kind. Only now did I notice something had healed me. Something extraordinary. Something Magical. My brother's ghost perchance?

Just as this thought crossed my mind, the radio stopped tuning in the station, and landed not upon song, but such as I took to be The War Report, until I realized just who it was that was speaking. As it was, however rousing and Soul-soaring and spirit-lifting his address in no short measure of his, so choice words, in full by to Skysong had been, I only heard his final words, as he said- '… in the clouds above our beaches, we will fight them!'

The static that followed, I thought ominous, as was that terrible feeling that suddenly came over me. Looking upon the vast array of flying machines just sat there in this morning's rising mist, I suddenly realized, I was never going to see these things again. That was when every single Skysong siren sounded in unison, and accord, orchestrating between themselves such a call to arms, even the dead were raised from their graves. I saw them all, converging upon the airfield runaways in the mist, the very ghosts of The Royal Magical Air Force past, here in the present, for the sake of England's future.

12

THE MOCKING BIRDS COME TO KILL

Spitfire became Dragon, and all soared into the sky.

Lancaster Bombers became Seagulls, and all soared into the sky.

Bristol Blenhiems became Albatross, and Eider Geese and all soared into the sky.

Air Arm Corsairs became Kestrels and Kingfishers, and all soared in their Squadrons into the sky.

Tomahawks became Sparrows and Bullfinches and Skylarks and Sparrowhawks, and all soared into the sky.

I watched a French Lafayette become a Firecrested bird of splendor and this, in its Squadron, I watched taking to the sky.

Hawker Hurricanes became Warblers and Woodpeckers and Goldcrests and Hawfinch, and all soared into the sky.

Vickers Wellingtons became Kestrels and Merlins and even still, there were many and more flying machines to become whatever Magical thing their pilot Wizards were known to manifest magnificently.

'Bird you coming? We're two gunners down!' hollered a disembodied voice I barely recognized behind the din of the Jinn of many engines, Merlin and more firing up upon this cold frosty morn.

SEPTEMBER 7TH 1940.

DAY ONE OF THE GERMANS, PUTTING ON THE BLITZ.

I joined the crew of the last bird to be scrambled for their were not enough pilots to pilot all of those idle flying machines we left behind to live to fly and fight another day, as soon as The Royal Magical Air Force found first and trained second, the next generation of young Wizards, Magicians, and Sorcerers to actually fly them; for most of those Wizards, Magicians, Sorcerers, and folks of an otherwise Otherworldly Enchanted ilk The Royal Magical Air Force had started this war with, were dead by now.

We were the last plane out upon this cold frosty misty morn, from whose mist my brother Claude made himself a thing for my eyes to see, but alas no other Wizards. I boarded a Lancaster, and though I inserted my wand into the receptacle beside the machine gun I took to, across fuselage from my brother, who needed no wand to loose ghostly rounds from that very real Browning machine gun his ghost took to; as it was, an Albatross our Avro Lancaster became, for luck I hoped.

Crew of seven souls, five, plus me, and seven counting Claude, my brother's ethereal morning mist-made ghost. He even seemed to smell of dew and freshly mown lawn. He took to the skylight, mid-upper turret

I went low, just back and beneath him.

This was my first time out as a gunner, mid-lower turret.

Browning machine gun x 2: 12.7 mm.

Capacity - Infinite make believe bullets.

Reload time: Irrelevant. Sky coverage: Poor.

Full Field of Vision: Obscured, until suddenly the fuselage around my position blended itself into a transparency akin to a steel but glass but really steel window upon world and sky for as far as I cared to cast my eyes, my mind, and my imagination out to sky.

I thought us surely performing a rear guard sky patrol action, when I realized we weren't hell-bound at the back of the beyond trail in the wake of our full force upon this day in The History of The World. But sure enough, the sky ahead of us, and below us for the most part, filled with the parting of a departing cloud, **RAVENS**.

Ruddy-muddy dozens upon dozens of them.

A whole **DARK FLOCK**. Behind the veil of the cloak of a shawl of ethereal illusion these things streamed into the sky sporting, **Messerschmitt**, a **WIZARD** and **BLACK** behind each one. We were Wizards and White, and this was all naught but chess. 'Checkmate!' I hollered as our Wizard in the pilot's cockpit dived-dived-dived so might we be the proverbial cat amongst the scattering pigeons as, before I knew it, all of our machine guns were singing in unison, in accord with this orchestration of pitch perfect song, the crescendo of which, an explosion of make believe bullets punching very real holes through our fuselage via the sky-strafing pass of a rogue errant RAVEN ace.

He'd been gunning specifically for Claude's gun this WIZARD, and surely would have decimated any living breathing soul caught in that gun bubble of a half-skylight my brother's ghost had been gunning from, had it been anyone but my brother.

Upon this Raven's pass, my brother blew the ruddy-muddy fiend out of the sky and laughed to see such fun I supposed as he made like a jolly good sport of it after the fact.

Finding myself momentarily having been distracted by this now passed peril, I turned back to my own piece of blue sky, ten thousand clear blue cloudless acres thereof as it seemed to me, and immediately found my instincts and every driven suddenly sense, to just open fire first, and then look, as opposed to any combat effective action I might have made to the contrary. A moment later, barely a half acre out to sky, a RAVEN disappeared right in front of me, blown to shredded smithereens by that barrage of make believe bullets I sent straight into that harm's way it flew straight into.

All throughout this battle it was machine gun work for me, my finger hardly even off the trigger for but a broken moment severed into two by this RAVEN or that RAVEN or all of the ruddy-muddy RAVENS in the sky. Of which there were surely hundreds, against just one Albatross and three whole Squadrons of Seagulls that came in from the direction of the bleak white sun, making of the sky, a veritable free-for-all.

This was dogfight! A dogfight to the death and to the victor no spoils save those flying machines saved, be that even, just the one airship making it back to Skysong, never to speak of this aerial engagement again.

Flak that was surely our own, bouncing us suddenly, I rocked within the cradle of my gunner's harness, losing my eye's fine purchase upon whatever piece of sky but suddenly found myself jerking to better swiftly align my machine guns with a careering *RAVEN*, one I didn't manage to stop taking a Seagull out of the sky, one this projectile ballistic *BIRD* literally cut in two, straight down the middle.

There were no parachutes deployed that I ever saw.

I know. I looked.

Surely outnumbered 3:1, but not outmatched, we filled the sky with our Magical tracers hoping that between ourselves, and so many Seagulls with so many guns crisscrossing Magic and make believe, we might just catch them all in the crossfire. Many and more we did, but still Seagulls were lost from thy sky. Some crashing and burning. Some just crashing. Some exploding entirely in the sky, others exploding upon the ground. And wherever it was above England we were, I could see enough of the distant patchwork ground painted in a hundred and one and more shades of green and fading gold, we were nowhere even close to being anywhere near the sky over London yet. But soon, and maybe, thereafter forever more, we would be?

Certainly we're still there even now, from a certain Magical point of view, given every image in the never ending stream of the unstoppable zoetrope, are in themselves, in being even just once upon a time, just static still life images, they must surely still exist, somewhere, some when.

This fight first though, back to it I guess, least I cut a long epic, arduous, terrible, bloodthirsty battle short, but then again, given this battle was so epic and bloodthirsty, and hours in the lasting, why would I ever do that?

Be here with me, right here, right now, inside this Avro Lancaster Bomber, listening to the imaginary make believe spell shells of imaginary make believe bullets, and these and their ghostly no less musically inclined sounding spent shells singing in percussive tandem around us. Like, tiny bells these Magical things. Ignoring those stowaway Fairies flitting around these cascading ethereal things, I continued with my barrage until forced to suddenly take my fingers from the triggers least I annihilated one of our own Seagulls, given the sudden careering turn out own pilot must have been forced into making.

All of our guns fell silent because of it.

My guns fell silent because of it, lower-mid fuselage.

My brother's guns, upper-mid fuselage, fell silent because of it.

The guns of the Wizard Pilot Officer Chester Butter-Spell in the tail turret, fell silent because of it.

The guns of the Wizard Pilot Officer Michael Wandland, nose turret, fell silent because of it.

All of us fell silent because of it, save our pilot in the cockpit, the Wizard, Flight Lieutenant, Lord Henry Cookooboro-Six-Smith. 'Close one chaps!' said this Wizard's voice in all of our headphones. 'Sorry about that.'

That said, we lost our tail turret entirely, for there where before this tail turret in a half-sky bubble of its own had been, now there was only sky.

That said, we lost our tail turret gunner too, entirely. For there where before had sat the Wizard Pilot Officer Chester Butter-Spell, now sat no one, only sky, only air.

Even our pilot took a bullet, and the Wizard Pilot Officer Michael Wandland in the nose turret, took two. This wounded man in need of my help, and so it came to pass, Fairies flitting around him though for all the help they were, they couldn't do much more than bathe him in their glow, I saw him to the floor mid-center fuselage, and did what I could by way of field dressing this Wizard's bloody wounds.

At least, I thought, he'd live. But he didn't.

All of our guns silent but for my brother's Browning machine guns, mid-upper turret, and thus only covering that upper turret scope of sky, we ran what I must surely now presume was a terrible gauntlet, our injuries thus far sustained, not to mention those to our Albatross surely cause for both concern, and reason enough to make of ourselves a Skysong sky-bound thing.

I knew why were weren't though. The answer to that question was obvious. Seeing as this was a fight to the death and the very last fighter plane in the sky, should we attempt to cut tail and run, those RAVENS able to do so, would chase us, all the way back to Skysong.

We couldn't risk the enemy bringing their rain with them, and thus, had no choice but to remain in the fight, for as long as we could remain in the fight.

I strapped my wounded man down to the floor of the fuselage and returned to my position behind the lower fuselage guns, such as afforded me clear sight of the sky beneath us, and wasted entirely, three RAVENS whilst Claude I thought got four before we both missed one and paid for it because of it. Upon me, for I let it come up from below, and on my brother, for he missed its first pass entirely.

That steel fuselage I'd fastened my wounded man to, gone, and gone entirely, for naught but a large hole remained where previously a wounded Wizard had been fastened, Wizard and chunk of fuselage both lost to the sky, I faltered in my duty, and my guns went silent.

'Sound off!' heckled the voice of our living breathing pilot in the cockpit. 'Who's still with me?'

'Bird sir!' I said into my microphone. 'It's just me and Claude sir.'

'Who the ruddy-muddy devil is Claude?' he asked.

'My brother sir!' I said to that, shouting over the thunder of the ongoing storm that was this theatre of sky battle, within which as it seemed to my ears of this dogfight, all was dogs barking in search of stones and bones to break the backs thereof.

'Thought your brother was dead Officer Bird?'

'Yes sir!' I said back to that. 'His ghost has been with me ever since sir! And his ghost is with us now sir! Mid-fuselage sir! Upper guns sir!'

'Right you are then Officer Bird,' he said. 'Keep it up old boy there's a good chap!'

'Aye-aye Captain!' I shouted back to that, throwing the rulebook out with the regulations where, or at least, by way of authorized and official radio chatter and Royal Magical Air Force speak was concerned.

'Wilco that man,' said the voice of the pilot. 'Roger. Message received and understood. Happy hunting. Over.'

'Bloody Wizard's going to get us all ruddy-muddy killed!' I procrastinated to my brother's ghost.

'I heard that. Over,' said our pilot to that.

'I know!' I shouted back. 'You were bloody meant to man!' I gunned for my life and got me two birds with one barrage of a thousand and one rounds and more surely, for they both crossed my path simultaneously and both paid the cost for it in full, with their lives.

And then, for us at least, that was that. I'd say we just lost feathers but as it was, our Albatross lost an entire wing and that, as I have said, or at least thus far suggested, was indeed that. Down our nose turned, and down out of the sky we fell, our entire Lancaster rattling so furiously, it actually began to shake itself to pieces, rear fin first.

I watched the fuselage disintegrating towards me, and then there I was, my parachute seemed to just open of its own accord, and I was rocking like a clock's pendulum a moment before my swing less brutal.

There was no second chute that I saw.

My wand I thought, realizing I no longer had it, so I drew instead that Luger I'd picked up from the kitchen table in the kitchen of a quaint little cottage in Cromley-Babberton, that I'd had upon me ever since, and cocked the trigger, my eyes upon this thing, before I finally thought to actually look up. And then down. And then all around me.

Everywhere I looked, I saw dogfight.

The sky was still thick with this battle's fury. And as it was, down through this fury I was descending, slowly but surely parachuting down over cloud as best as I could see. Just cloud beneath me, and still so much sky to fall through before I'd ever hit the cloud below, suddenly told me we'd been very high in the sky indeed when our Lancaster Seagull finally bowed out of the carnage.

Be this just one of life's moments, I took my fill.

How could I not? Given my predicament.

Would I, or wouldn't I, be spotted? That was the question. The second question that also sprang to mind being that of a question of, presumably having first been spotted, what then would whomever spotted me, choose to do about it?

Down through this sky filled with dogfight I drifted.

Aimless like a cloud.

Just watching, unable to do ought but watch, least I close my eyes and see from this moment on, only black. But no, no I would not close my eyes, not when the sky, never more visceral in my mind, was filled with so many wonderful things to see. In my peril, I saw the sublime, and peril became poetry became for those RAVENS I witnessed de-feathered, a poetic poison.

Did I laugh to see such fun?

And so tempt thy fate in doing so?

A good few minutes I was descending before I hit the cloud, and thus found myself falling thereafter straight through it, only to realize not only did I still have half the sky to fall, but I was plummeting down through said sky, trailing a shredded parachute behind me.

I released this chute in tatters and watched it soaring away upon new winds entirely as I continued to tumble and then turn in the air so as to face my fate beneath me. It was mostly cloud, denying me true sight of my true height as I plummeted, but I would not yet release my secondary chute until I at least had the bare minimum of sky needed to land alive from so reckless a halo fall.

Down through the cloud I soared, like a stone.

Down through the cloud until suddenly I caught a glimpse of sky and immediately pulled my rip-chord as my heart hit my throat, and not a praying man, nor ever a praying man, I suddenly found myself praying with all of my might as suddenly I jerked like a thing caught by that open chute above me, that caught me, five, four, three, two, one second before I impacted the surface of the lake beneath the battle above.

Whoosh went the water as down-down-down my own fury took me, deeper and deeper into the black before I even thought to release the parachute I was still wearing. And *oh*, was it ever cold!

I thought myself dead, and wondered why I wasn't dead?

I thought myself dead, and wondered why I wasn't dead?

I thought myself dead, and wondered why I wasn't dead?

I watched the black enclosing upon me upon all sides, and then the black was above me and only getting blacker as I sank deeper and deeper into the darkness of the depths of this lake; not a lake I care to name given that which I was to see down there, is probably still down there. Black all around me, I looked down, to see the black beneath me growing slowly less black, and less black even still, until I saw what the source of the ghostly ominous golden light was, that I thought treasure for sure, and treasure it was, of a certain kind.

There were downed bombers at the bottom of the lake, within one of which, were trapped Fairies for sure I thought, and Fairies there were, for I swam to this sunken Lancaster Seagull, just a sunken Lancaster bomber now, and swimming in through a hole in its underside, I came up for air within, to find myself bathed in the light of those Fairies imprisoned by this air-pocket. Given everyone knows Fairies can't swim, nor hold their breath much at all, I trust I need say no more than that, to fully impart to thee, thine and these Fairies plights, for I already knew, even if they did not, they were all going to either drown, or asphyxiate, no two ways about it, one way or another, all of these Fairies were already dead.

Even as I held myself there, in this moon-pool of sorts, above which the Fairies formed a spectral sun, themselves treading air-pocket like I was treading water in the belly of the bomber I'd found them within, the water level rose a few inches. Some hairline fracture leaking air somewhere, and this bomber slowly sinking into the mud of the lake bed, I swam to fuselage wall and pulled myself up out of the water into the air-pocket itself.

Fairies flitted around me, and I could sense they sensed their own doom coming, maybe not soon, but soon enough to be for these Fairies so full of light and life, too soon. Too soon for these English Fairies by far, the mortality of them there to be seen in their trembling dispositions.

I shared the crumbs of a chocolate-coated wafer bar I just so happened to find in one of my pockets, and so it was, we between ourselves allowed an hour, and then two, and then three come to pass, within which time, the water level wasn't much more than a half-foot higher than it had been. I thought I might spend the whole night with them, slowly but surely freezing to death, until I thought I might make a fire, before I thought just how stupid an idea that actually was. But as it played out, though I only entertained this ridiculous notion for but a split second, within this second it occurred to me just what it was I'd need to actually be able to light a fire in the first place.

Though my wand was lost, it was always possible a

standard-issue, military-grade, Royal Magical Air Force wand was still present upon this sunken bomber. If there was, then I set my sights upon the goal of finding it, but there wasn't one above me to be found, not in the pilot's cockpit or in the nose cone. Nor did those machine guns upper and lower mid-fuselage, actually inspected underwater, have their affiliated wands still in-place. And the sheer absence of bodies of any kind, made me think the crew of this Lancaster Seagull had actually all lived to bail out.

Ruddy-muddy lucky sods!

I had to resurface for air, of which I took a lung full, if not two lungs full, before I dived down into the tail gunner's half-bubble, and low and behold, retrieved from that machine gun there, the only wand to be left on-board.

I surfaced with it in my hand with great expectations, and joy, great expectations and joy, for surely with this wand, though I knew little enough of its true Magic, or its purpose, and power, nay mention what million and one other uses a Wizard might have or be able, via the wit of the Wizard himself, or herself, to find whatever alternative use for this thing, this thing might else otherwise be good for. This thing that was a wand, and I was after all, was I not, a Wizard?

I found myself wondering yet again, what is a Wizard?

With the wand in my hand, its writ the same-same as I'd ever seen before seeing as it was standard issue this wand.

IN THE NAME OF THE KING

&

BY ROYAL DECREE & APPOINTMENT TO THE KING

'In the name of The King,' I said, flourishing this thing with only one thought held perfectly in my mind. More of an image really, that of this bomber rising up out of the depths to break once more this lake's surface. And thus, it was so. We rose up, slowly, and though I thought no sooner was the nose cone free of the water, the Fairies would all fly away, they didn't. Instead they flocked around the nose cone machine guns, the triggers specifically, and proceeded to get back into the fight, firing from the nose cone Browning twin machine guns, imaginary make believe, Fairy-conjured, bullets.

I climbed for my part into the pilot's seat, and inserting the wand into that receptacle designed specifically to receive this thing, I reared us out of the water, unaware I was also salvaging from the depths two other equally ruined formed of Lancaster bombers trailing pond weed and pond rags, both of which proceeded to follow us into the sky, the battle done and gone now, as we three planes, piloted only by me, least Claude was in one of the others, and all of the guns of these three Lancaster Bombers manned by Fairies, we headed for London, upon this night on earth, September 7th 1940.

Unfortunately for London on this night, we were too late.

Need I say more? For what picture might I better paint for thee in thy mind's eye but to say, be thee able to see anything of an imaginary nature with thy mind's eye at all? See flames, for that is all there was to be seen of London on this night: Flames!

13

SWALLOWS & DRAGONS: OPERATION SKYSONG (OR) BYE-BYE BERLIN

The briefing we received back at Skysong, where we Pilot Officers were concerned, given that we needed only concern ourselves with little, was brief: In retaliation for the bombing of London, we were bombing **Berlin**.

The Royal Magical Air Force & The Royal Air Force together at the same time, so might we hide our Magical bombs behind our more mundane ones, just like the ruddy-muddy Germans had done.

This was really it this time. This really was the war we hoped would never come.

'Bye-bye Berlin,' someone said to me upon the way out, all

of us Pilot Officers excused from the continuation of the briefing on-mass, leaving all higher ranking Royal Magical Air Force Wizards to discuss, in further, and much more closed, but not clandestine, council, the further subtle nuances and finer details of the Mission, from The Magical Air Marshal to the last few surviving Flying Officers.

I stopped dead in my tracks, and looked at this fresh faced well-groomed new recruit of a fellow who most likely only had training hours upon training wheels under the radar's blip so far so good in his life. He couldn't have been much older than either eighteen or nineteen years old, and though I was not much older- myself than seventeen and a half, I wasn't half as fresh faced and wick as these Wizards still wet behind the ears were, and wanting, and wanting of not just luck alone where the fates and the combined fortunes of these fellows was concerned.

All would need stouthearted angels over their shoulders in the guise of the gals, The Royal Magical Air Force's damsels for dames in The War Room, & The Map Room, or whatever room of Strategic Magic Air Command required said damsels for dames to man like these vital stations could be trusted to no other.

Given it was a bombing run, we'd all be flying bombers.

Seagulls, and Eider Geese, and Albatross, and Dragon.

Not a praying man, nor ever a praying man, but for that one time that seemed at the time to actually pay off in aces, I will admit to thee now, so long now after the fact, I actually prayed that I wouldn't find myself assigned to a Bomber that sported a single one of these fresh faced heroes whose eyes seemed already to sport the glory of those medals these wick Wizards were clearly hoping to win. The air of this around them was palpable.

The air around me, was one of naught but pity.

I knew. They did not.

I'd already seen. Their eyes had seen nothing so good so far at this point in their lives.

I'd already been there and back, and they'd never even left Skysong before now.

I knew what to expect. Their expectations I already knew, knew nothing of the horrors of battle to come; for they already thought the battle won, having fought it already in their minds having had not much more than a few minutes to think about it. Ruddy-muddy fools I thought. I could see it all there in their eyes and their actions to be seen to be gleamed from these boisterous slap-happy shy-boy flyboy barrack-crib backseat hotshots.

And not an ace up their single sleeve.

Is this what we've been reduced to I wondered to myself. For nothing to me seemed or sang truer than that idea that passed through my mind as I stood there, watching all of them wandering away still with kick enough in their strides to appear all but dancing off into the bleak murky haze of the sheer absence of reason, or even reasonable doubt where these immortal fools were concerned. All thought they would live forever. I even heard one or two of them say as much, more fool them, for never is fate more tempted, than when thee tempts thy fate, thyself.

Do say never, and mean it!

These fools didn't even know what it was they were saying, even when I heard them transgressing upon those orders to the contrary we'd all been given, to repeat nothing, and say nothing to nobody about those things we'd all just been briefed upon, in so far as we needed to be briefed upon such things.

I gave these idiots a piece of my mind, but as our ranks were comparable and experience in their eyes didn't seem to count for much, they damn near blindsided my comments, but all snapped to attention when my gal appeared from the sidelines of this staged theatre of fools whose backdrop better breeding than just the plain good old common sense of England's common everyman.

The lions are become lambs I thought.

I already knew because of this, we would be flying into a slaughter.

'Officer Bird,' she said, her eyes upon everyone but me. 'I trust, as you have some time before this night ends true. You'll impart to those new recruits who look like they need it if you ask me, a little of your combat expertise. You are after all, where confirmed kills are concerned, Skysong's number one Air Combat Ace.' She smiled, and then added for the record- 'Uncontested for months.'

A few wick Wizards cottoned on quick, and quicker than others for their part, and upon the part played by others, which was The Fool, not at all.

'No promises,' I said, not meaning to sound so dismissive, but it translated thus regardless.

'Oh, Officer Bird,' she added like an afterthought. 'Arthur I mean. Are we still on for tonight as planned?'

'As planned?' I questioned, unaware we actually had any plans as we hadn't, most lately, even seen each other to actually speak in the first place.

'Tonight. Midnight. Picnic in the moonlight. Our secret field. And Arthur- Let's make it our little secret.'

If she said this just to earn me that respect in the eyes of wick Wizards she felt I was owed, deserved, and due, she said the right thing, for her words had their desired effect. After all, the most beautiful dame in all of Skysong Manor just proved herself mine. She winked at me, smiled upon the back of an airborne kiss, one she launched through the air from where she stood, sending this projectile thing in my direction, and actually, given a Wizard she was, was my gal, leaving wet red lips imprinted upon my cheek forever more, or at least, seeing as I departed upon this bombing run still sporting this kiss, for as long as I had left yet to live.

Midnight I thought to myself.

I ought to have been sleeping. But then again, I wouldn't sleep. I don't think anyone would, especially those few good men of the ground crew teams that had been ordered to work through the night so as to have every single flying machine in our armada combat ready and ready for the great off, no later than late morning.

Many Magical things I will make no further mention of, assisted them in this regard.

Try to imagine it if you can, for I certainly couldn't.

Outside the manor doors I took the air, until finally I found myself in the Officer's mess tent, with not a familiar face anywhere to be seen despite their being hundreds of us. I ate alone, a hearty portion of whatever it was that was served on that night, and then found myself wandering to, but ultimately walking right on past those deckchairs sat in the shade of familiar trees, for I recognized not a single face sat within a single one of them. Those same deckchairs where once upon a time, and for many nights and more, but now seemingly never again, I'd known such mirth and merriment with men who were Wizards once, but all were dead men now.

I checked my watch, it was 2200 hrs.

One sleep till **Berlin** I thought, and then… 'Excuse me sir! Sir! Are you Bird sir? I mean, Pilot Officer Bird sir? The one who has a ghost on his shoulder sir?'

'What is it?' I asked, saying only this.

'Officer Pilot Bird sir?'

'As you say. Now what do you want? Get on with it lad I haven't got all ruddy-muddy night.'

'Wing Commander Raven Mocker requests an-'

'Raven Mocker?' I questioned, this name a name it felt like I hadn't heard for seven lifetimes of Skysong at least.

'Wing Commander Raven Mocker sir. He asks that you

join him at the gate to Skysong Manor, sir.'

'Gate?' I questioned. 'You mean the manor house doors?'

'Sorry sir. Gate sir. If you take my meaning sir?'

'Gate?' I questioned again. 'What ruddy-muddy- Oh, you mean the main gate don't you?'

'As you say sir.'

'What the ruddy-muddy devil is the Wing Commander doing at the main gate?'

'Didn't say sir. Don't know sir. Will that be all sir?'

'Go on,' I told him. 'Go get some sleep.'

'Sleep?' he questioned, like a thing so wired he intended to remain awake for the rest of his life, never seeking this distraction called sleep ever again, at least where the prime of his life so far so good was concerned.

'Sleep tonight, and maybe tomorrow you'll live to die some other time. Take thee no sleep at all tonight lad. And you can be sure after tomorrow, you'll be dead and some other poor unfortunate soul will have your bunk, your best mug, and your Strategic Air Command damsel.'

'Yes sir- I'll see I at least try sir.'

'Make sure you do. If I find you on my crew tomorrow, asleep at your post- I'll shoot you.'

He must have seen it in my eyes, that I wasn't fooling around with him, that I really meant it. 'And if I try and find I can't sleep sir?'

'Try harder,' I told him, and that said, I walked away so he wouldn't have to, and besides, who was this ruddy-muddy fresh-faced wick fool that I should end up looking into the back of him, and not he mine?

I found as advised, Wing Commander Raven Mocker, code name in case of capture in case you've forgotten, for this man's real world name, albeit Magic world, which as far as he was concerned was the only world there was, seeing as the mundane folks could hardly be said to live in the real world at all for their parts played in this great theatre of life, the very stage thereof that world beneath thy feet wherever it is thy feet walk thee. Mine had walked me all the way to Skysong Manor's main gate, a two mile walk from the ruddy-muddy front door as it turned out; the last time I'd ever transgressed this road's gravel, actually following the road in reverse, from gate to door in a stolen jeep, as opposed to having walked it this time, door to gate as it was.

Raven Mocker, was Jennifer-Jane Songbird's uncle. He told me as much and this perhaps explained her fondness for me, seeing as it was I who saved this man's life once upon a time. A favorite uncle of hers no doubt, no less. We spoke little though his eyes said a lot. He thanked me. He heard out my account of his baptism by fire, and his salvation therefrom the flames thereof, and that said, there really wasn't much else to be said between us. I knew this man no better than he knew me, though I'm sure he'd asked around and asked to see my combat efficiency reports, and confirmed kill count I imagine. Surely naught but these TOP SECRET – EYES ONLY reports had thus inspired him to come to me with a proposition.

Seemed The Royal Magical Air Force were putting together an equally TOP SECRET branch of The Magical Strategic Air Arm tree. And no, unfortunately I don't mean that arm of The Royal Magical Ministry of Air Defense that evolved into England's Secret Space Program, but that arm of The Royal Magical Air Force that for the remained of the war, would not be concerning itself with fighting the enemy in the sky over our beaches, nor taking the war to those cities teeming with thy enemy's shepherd's mundane German sheep, be they bleating for their new master or not: **Jawohl. Rein Sir. Drei taschen voller Herr**; which is to say- Yes sir. No sir. Three bags full sir.

Wing Commander Raven Mocker would be attacking the enemy's **COVENS**, wherever it was these **SECRET LAIR'S** of **THE ENEMY BEAST** were hidden beyond all plain sight, be these things hidden in plain sight or not. Regardless, once they'd been located, they would be bombed into oblivion. No bombs barred!

'So what do you say lad?' he asked me, starting up the engine of what I thought most likely my jeep. 'Are you in? Say yes and you can jump right in and never look back.'

'Can't sir. Needed sir. Bombing Berlin tomorrow sir.'

'When you get back then. I'll send a jeep for you.'

'As you say sir,' I said to that. 'When I get back.'

'So you're in- Flight Lieutenant Bird?'

'Yes sir!' I said to that, seeing as this next step up the Royal Magical Air Force ladder came with a promotion to boot. 'I'm in.'

'Drop a bomb for me son,' he told me, and that said, he sped off and I never saw him again.

I checked my watch. It was 2400 hrs. Midnight.

Jennifer-Jane!

I ran, the whole two miles back to Skysong before detouring off towards that wall into fields kissed by a full midnight moon, thinking I'd have to double-time it to the trees only to hear a voice in the moonlight that stopped me dead. 'You didn't go with him then?' she said softly.

'How could I,' I told her.

'Strings were pulled. I thought to spare you tomorrow's bombing run Arthur.'

'I wasn't thinking about that,' I told her, softly.

'Were you thinking Arthur?'

'Only of right here. Right now,' I told her, given that is where I was, heart, mind, Soul, bones and stones and all. Just for that kiss I had not yet summoned nor plucked up the courage or the nerve I needed perchance to either steal this kiss, or purchase said kiss from her at whatever cost she cared to levy against its priceless worth to thee.

'Oh Arthur,' she protested. 'What have I done.'

'Only that which was necessary,' I said. 'For I would not have yielded this night and its moon gladly, knowing you were stood here beneath it alone without me.'

And then she kissed me.

I awoke at the first light of day, upon a picnic blanket, upon our field, a single green apple wet from the morning dew sat upon that picnic basket she had left, this thing the only thing to say she'd ever been here in the first place.

At least I thought, we'll always have last night's stars.

Rising, I took the apple and ate it upon my walk back to Skysong, arriving upon the airfield to discover the mission had been brought forward and already engines by the ground crews were being warmed up in combat effective readiness for the great off.

It was going to be a huge offensive. A monumental air armada the like of sky had not seen sported this far by its own home team, such as would be playing away today, England Vs Germany. An eye for an eye to leave the whole world blind, and scratching around in the dark for an Age more, always for just one more Age, until maybe, just maybe… War being war whose rug, that ties naught but the cold cruel hearth of thy enemy of all mankind's castle's keepsake together, you'll find, once lifted, has room for much and more to be simply swept beneath this thing's blanket indifference: War being war: Within which, born upon the back of which, forgiveness after the fact is due none but The Hangman.

I thought my house in order, for I still sported last night's stars in my head and in my heart, where every single shooting star we saw, be they shooting stars or V2 rockets or what-not or whatever, had ended up. I walked bathed in a flitting Fairy's soft golden glow, myself informed telepathically by this messenger

Fairy just which Bomber I'd been assigned to, and in just what capacity: PILOT.

Plane Ident:

The universe's living breathing sense of humor, or someone else's I wondered? I couldn't even tell if that was a good fortune or not, regardless, I had my bird, my wand, and even from a distance I could see her from a whole airfield away. I made my way straight to her, and found my gunners, and my flight crew ready willing and good to go. Likely lads the lot of them.

'Fairy flying with us too today sir?' someone said.

'Not if she has any sense,' I said to that.

'Come again sir?' said another.

'Fairy don't need no death wish to get herself killed in this day and Age Pilot,' I told this Royal Magical Air Force fresh-faced wick wet behind the ears not long since last mothered recruit.

'Killed sir?'

'Bombing run this sir ain't it sir?'

'Berlin and back right sir?'

'Surprise attack I was told sir.'

Pilot, plane, sky I thought, but as it was I waited for my four wick Wizards for this magnificent flying machine's machine gunners to all have their wick word, before I looked once at my more-experienced than thou long-serving Flight Officers, all two of them, and afforded these two worldly-wise Wizards a nod before my eyes back on those grassroots, so freshly seeded, they hadn't even started sprouting shoots yet. 'We'll encounter their fighters long before we see Berlin boys,' I told them. 'Ravens, Crows, Blackbirds, Banshees, Bats, Mocking Birds and more.'

'And more sir?'

'By the time we reach Berlin,' I said, supposing at a best guess, though I didn't really know what it was I was talking about, I was at least, best guess, ball park. 'The sky will be so full of their Dragons, we won't see Berlin beneath us for the backs of those Dragons that are.'

Hard to truly say really whether what follows next is long-story-short, or short-story-long to be honest. After all, what do you need to know?

I looked up at our brand new Lancaster Bomber to see someone, more than likely some artist within the ground crews had painted a Vargas-esque rendition of my star-crossed-gal, Jennifer-Jane, beneath whose beauty, sat aback a bomb, she appeared to be saying, at least according to the caption, words I wouldn't myself ever have placed as having been born of her lips.

'We'll meet again'

I already knew that it was a lie.

I looked at my fellow crewmen and just hoped we'd sell

our lives as dearly as I hoped we just might. 'All right!' I said. 'Who do we have here?' I looked upon my gunners like I might be inspecting them, when really, all I was expecting of these dead men walking, soon to be dead men flying in their very own coffin with wings, straight into **HELL ON EARTH**, little more than that.

Pilot Officer Winston Spellby,' said the Wizard Winston Spellby. 'Tail gunner sir.'

Pilot Officer Charlie Spellslinger,' said the Wizard Charlie Spellsinger. 'Nose cone gunner sir.'

Pilot Officer George Snow-Spell,' said the wick Wizard George Snow-Spell. Mid-upper gunner sir.'

Pilot Officer Emanuel Spellsong,' said the wick Wizard Emanuel Spellsong. 'Mid-lower, gunner sir.'

'What did they do?' I scoffed without actually meaning to. 'Assign you to me via alphabetical order?'

'Aye sir,' said one of my Flight Officers.

'Most likely,' said the other.

'Well, ruddy-muddy Spell-fire and hymn-stone,' I grumbled. 'Hell of a thing to go placing the fates of all us in a fool's fool's errand as just such a that. Regardless. I'm Arthur Bird. And these fine chaps here are Flight Officers Wands-Worth and Kipling.' The wind wept I thought to myself, as it crossed my mind to consider, but said nothing concerning that one simple inalienable truth currently ringing in my mind with ten thousand familiar bells and more: The **FOKKER-WOLVES** wouldn't let us get within a hundred miles of **Berlin**, without first selling to us their every single acre of sky at such a cost, we'd never afford the return fare, should we even live to make it that far into this presumably one way mission in the first place?

It was just a shame, that for all of the few hundred fresh-faced wick Wizards too wick to be considered Warriors yet, this mission was undoubtedly going to be their first, and their last. None of us were coming back alive from this I thought. Just as long as enough of us made it to **Berlin** to bomb the ruddy-muddy City back to The Dark Ages, we could all go to Heaven and rest assured forever more, our final Mission in **THE WAR** was a raging firestorm of a success, one to rival the very sacking of Rome itself, once upon a time.

Once sat within my cockpit pilot's seat, I slipped my wand into its fixture, as did all of the Wizards onboard do the same. The gunners with their wands brought their Browning machine guns to life, and my Flight Officers got their flight stations into Magical order. No disguise this time. No ethereal cloak of a Fantastic Magic shawl within the mirage of which we might hide from mundane eyes, on the contrary, as planned by The Magical Royal Air Force we would be flying, no doubt someone's idea of either a joke, or a dastardly deception designed to hopefully trick those Squadrons upon Squadrons upon Squadrons of **FOKKER-WOLVES** guarding Berlin if not Germany's skies in full, to just thick us mundane things and therefore, by the distinction of those Secret Pacts and duly signed Armistice Accords the historical account of WWII make no historical account thereof, we might just be left to Germany's more mundane **Luftwaffe**.

Once in the sky and having attained our pre-assigned cruising altitude and attitude, we joined a vast sky flock of hundreds of flying machines. Both Royal Magic and just plain mundane Air Force. Berlin and back the only thing currently upon everyone's minds I supposed, just as this bird's internal radio searched seemingly of its own accord, for whatever choice song currently being broadcast by English free radio.

It was playing 'I'll Never Smile Again', by Tommy Dorsey & His Orchestra, with Frank Sinatra & The Pied Pipers providing this song's refrain. Not necessarily perfect I thought, but at least it was poignant, despite the tempo of the song and the melancholy maudlin mood it put all on-board this Bomber in.

'You mind sir if we leave it playing?' asked one so wick he didn't even know our call signs nor a single word of our regulation radio speak: Officer Pilot Spellslinger most likely, be any of my wick Wizards actually fully fledged Officer Pilots and not just the next best Pilot Cadets fast-tracked their wings so might they fly along with this otherwise ill-equipped ill-provisioned ill-advised, in-the-heat-of-the-moment decision, to pay the ruddy-muddy German back for supposedly accidentally MAGICALLY bombing London by mistake.

What these MAGICAL bombs had otherwise been meant for never even coming into it.

'Only as far as The White Cliffs,' said I over the plane-wide intercom. 'We'll listen to The War Report as we cross The Channel, and then it's radio silence chaps,' I said. 'And do please remember to turn your radios off gentleman. And if you can't remember to do that. When we reach France, either throw your radio out, or throw yourself out. Either way I'll be hearing not a word from anyone until I say we're all free to speak once more. Over.'

'When will that be sir? Over,' said Spellby.

'When the ruddy-muddy enemy knows we're either coming, or having bombed Berlin back to basics, the enemy cottons on to that fact that we're already on our way home. Over,' I said to that, and that said, I let the chaps listen to the music of English free radio and turned for tuning my mind back into that job I had both to hand, and in hand I supposed, all being well, and if not well then hopefully better; we'd make it in one piece to Berlin, bomb it, and make it back with all of my chaps alive, with a flying machine at least in such a condition, it might yet fly again some other sunny day.

That I thought, was going to take a Miracle.

And the odds of it being my plane afforded the inevitable Miracle, the one Miracle that at least one plane usually can count upon, was as best as I could tell, 100:1.

It wasn't **Berlin** and back. It was **Berlin** or bust.

I felt I'd already used up all of my fated luck just to make it this deep into the war. Why they made me pilot and not somebody else, anybody else, I had no idea, short of there actually not having been anyone else to fill these pilot's shoes. As it was, all I had to do was fly.

So we flew, over England, over The White Cliffs of Dover,

over France, and into Germany as we bounced upon flak seemingly all the way to **Berlin!**

I won't much wax lyrical now.

We bombed **Berlin**: End of; I won't say ought else about that, save to say, in bombing **Berlin**, **Berlin** burned *and oh* did it ever burn so brightly.

'Well ain't any of us getting into Heaven now,' I said, breaking radio silence since the last time I broke radio silence, by which time, it didn't really matter. As it was, I looked out into the sky, and saw the sky filling with them.

Hundreds upon hundreds upon hundreds of them. Like locusts these fiendish flying machines of a choice MAGICAL disposition DARKLY indeed.

Finally, the enemy WIZARDS were come.

FOKKER-WOLVES!

&

DRAGON!

Strict disciplinarian BEASTS one and all.

They filled the sky: Perhaps we'll die.

It all came to an end for my Lancaster Bomber when it exploded, leaving me hurtling through the air, my wand still in my hand, flaming flak all around me, night above me, and naught but an ocean of flames beneath me, the sky filled with more black smoke than sky itself.

Did I mean to take off without a parachute?

Down through the sky I plummeted, making of myself a Phoenix for effect, casting this Fantastical Magical apparition of an ethereal mirage of an incandescent guise about my stones and my bones as I plummeted. Reaching with my flightless wings that were my arms that were my wings, soaring like a stone if not precisely like a stone, one that cannot soar but fall, straight down, no two ways about that.

DRAGON & FOKKER-WOLVES I fell straight past.

At which I marveled to see such things so up close and so personal. As you can no doubt imagine, it really was quite the thing to see, and as I fell down through the heights of the sky, I saw it all, and lived a life larger than any life I might otherwise have imagined for myself. After all, as I'm sure you've no doubt guessed already, what with **Berlin** burning beneath me, with nothing but the flames of **Berlin** to break my fall, it was quite the Zen inducing experience.

All was serene. All was sublime.

Finally, just before I died, I actually learned how to fly.

Finally, just before I died, I truly came to understand just what it was that made a Wizard, a Wizard.

THE END?

Printed in Great Britain
by Amazon